LORD, I HAVE A QUESTION

Story Devotions for Girls

BETTY WESTROM SKOLD

AUGSBURG Publishing House • Minneapolis

LORD, I HAVE A QUESTION

Copyright © 1979 Augsburg Publishing House

Library of Congress Catalog Card No. 79-50079

International Standard Book No. 0-8066-1718-7

Cover design and cover illustration: Koechel-Peterson Design

Illustrations: Becca Martinson

Scripture quotations unless otherwise noted are from the Revised Standard Version of the Bible, copyright 1946, 1952, and 1971 by the Division of Christian Education of the National Council of Churches. TEV stands for Good News Bible: Today's English Version, copyright 1966, 1971, and 1976 by American Bible Society.

For Bill,
who trusted me to become
the mother of his children

About This Book

Have you ever noticed how you sail through some days as easily as a Frisbee? Those are the days you find two good answers for every small problem. But on other days your spirits droop like a broken umbrella. Something's bothering you. No matter how many times you try to poke that feeling down, it keeps bobbing back to the surface. That's the day you need a friend.

In this book you'll meet girls about your age, some from the city, some from small towns, and some from the farm. There are girls who like basketball and others who enjoy weaving or playing guitar. The girls in these stories aren't perfect. They're real people who get into fights with their brothers and take bubble gum cards with them to church. But they all have one thing in common. They all have those "broken umbrella" days.

Each story begins with a question, a question you may have thought about on a day when things were going wrong. I hope that as you read the stories you may see in them a reflection of yourself, that you'll stop every once in a while and think, "Y'know, she's a lot like me." You won't find yourself on every page. Some of the girls' problems may not be your problems at all. But why not read them anyway? They may give you a helpful idea to pass along to a friend.

Don't ever forget that God keeps track of you in your troubles. Sometimes God's help comes to you through a teacher, sometimes through your parents or through a friend. Sometimes God speaks to you directly through your Bible. The Bible verse and prayer at the end of each story are meant to help you form the habit of bringing your everyday problems to the Lord, who is your friend.

If this book touches you in any real way, you should know that I've been helped in putting it together.

Special thanks go to my own daughter, Carol Skold Uecker, who is always both cheerleader and critic for all my writing projects. Besides, Carol's own growing years lie hidden in a lot of these stories.

Thanks also to Lasse Stohl, my pastor and friend, for encouragement and wise counsel, and to Wes and Corrine Lindstrom and Linda Stolhanske for parents' insights.

For other background help I am grateful to school teachers and administrators in Sauk Centre, Minnesota: Chuck and Anita Hellie, Mona Kohorst, Harold

Nelson, Larry Sorenson, Wes Frank, Sidney Kjeldahl, and Carolyn Trettle.

But most of all, thank you to four girls—Andrea Stolhanske, Kelly Delaney, Jennifer Lindstrom, and Kara Bren—for sharing their lives with me and helping to make the stories real.

It Just Takes One

The kids really get wild in science class. I feel sorry for the teacher, but if I don't act like everybody else I'm afraid I won't have any friends. Is that wrong?

"Could any of you girls tell me who did that to the chairs?"

Laurie looked up from her chiliburger into the face of the supervising teacher. Then she glanced over to the far end of the lunchroom and saw the swaying tower of plastic chairs that almost reached the ceiling.

Like the other girls at her table, Laurie just looked back at Mrs. Gentry with a sober "how-should-I know?" face. But of course she did know. Everybody knew. Mrs. Gentry sighed and took her question to the next table.

"Now look what he's doing," Julie said in a loud whisper. They all looked back to where Andy Thompson was sitting. He had grabbed the catsup container and was squirting a gooey, looping ribbon all over the polished surface of the table.

Then, seeing Mrs. Gentry, Andy got to his feet, punched Bill Slattery on the shoulder, and picked up his tray to leave. About 20 feet from the trash barrel, he crumpled his milk carton and lobbed a perfect long shot into the garbage. Then he walked out of the lunchroom, trampling on Sidney Craig's heels as he went.

All the girls around Laurie shook their heads and grinned. "Andy really is terrible," Julie said, as they gathered up their trays. "He's always showing off. But he really is kind of funny."

Far down the hall Laurie could see him walking along, followed by a gang of his special friends, slamming locker doors as he went.

When Andy Thompson moved into town from Clark's Corner, he seemed to bring trouble right through the school door with him. Andy was someone you couldn't help but notice. He was easily the tallest boy in the class, his hair was thick and black, and he always wore denim jackets with his jeans. In gym class he was the only one who could do one-handed pushups. Andy had a reckless laugh, and he always called parents and teachers by their first names.

Wherever Andy went he seemed to set off sparks, but he was at his worst in Mrs. Gentry's science class.

13

Maybe it was because Mrs. Gentry spoke softly, or maybe he had heard that this was her first year of teaching. Andy seemed to delight in tormenting her.

It had been going on since the first day of school. That day Mrs. Gentry couldn't get her own microscope to focus. At first she just seemed uneasy about it. Then she panicked, telling the class they'd better go back to their seats and read the first chapter in the textbook. Laurie had noticed the secret fear in her teacher's eyes, and she'd said a little silent prayer that Mrs. Gentry would have better luck with the microscope the next day.

From that day on Andy Thompson was trouble for Mrs. Gentry. He made crazy bunny shadows on the screen whenever classroom films were being shown. He folded the first paper airplane, but before long everybody was doing it, and there was a blizzard of them. And who but Andy could have arranged the waste-basket bouquet while Mrs. Gentry was writing on the chalkboard? He tiptoed up to her desk, pulled the clump of weeds from the brown jug, transplanted them into the wastebasket, and poked a plastic pennant from the burger shop into the middle of the bouquet. Then he sneaked back to his seat in the front row before Mrs. Gentry knew what was happening.

Not everyone admired him, but they all laughed when he pulled a trick. And everybody felt just a little bit braver when he was around. Soon Mitzie was blowing big, quivering balloons of bubble gum, and

Scott was tipping way back in his chair, and Laurie was passing notes.

One day a crowd of kids gathered around Andy at the end of the hall, right outside of Mrs. Gentry's door. Laurie could see that Andy was doing all the talking. They all listened, nodded, then exploded into laughter. Laurie started to go into the room, but Melissa pulled at her sleeve. "Laurie, c'mere," she said. She explained Andy's plan.

As soon as Mrs. Gentry had finished taking roll, Andy would get up to sharpen his pencil, and that would be the signal for the walkout. Everybody would get up together and walk right out the door, out the side exit of the school, and gather back of the storage building. Some six-packs of Coke were hidden there, and they'd just goof off until time to catch the bus home. It was important to take Mrs. Gentry by surprise, and the trick would work only if everybody was in on it.

"But why?" Laurie asked. "I mean, what has Mrs. Gentry. . . . Are you sure that—"

The faces around her darkened with disapproval, and Laurie's timid protest withered and died. "Well, OK, I guess if everybody else. . . . OK, I guess I'll do it." Andy looked pleased.

Going into the classroom, Laurie stopped at the teacher's desk to hand in her make-up work. Mrs. Gentry smiled and asked if she was feeling better now. Why did she have to be so nice? Laurie wasn't feeling better at all. She'd rather go to the orthodontist and have her braces tightened than walk out that door with the others. Was there any way out of it? No. She had promised.

The trick worked. Mrs. Gentry called the roll, and Andy popped up from his seat and strolled toward the pencil sharpener. Then everybody else picked up their books and walked out without a word.

Behind the storage building, they laughed as they remembered the look on Mrs. Gentry's face. What would the principal say when he heard about it? What else would be fun to try?

Laurie handed her Coke can to Julie. "Want the rest of this? I feel sort of full."

When the big yellow buses began rolling up to the school, Laurie started in the direction of No. 9. Then she remembered. If she hurried, there should be time to pick up her permission slip for Friday's field trip. She slipped quickly through the after-school confusion to the principal's office. Nobody was at the front desk, so she waited by the bulletin board, glancing at the notices.

From the inner office Laurie could hear someone talking on the telephone. It was Mrs. Gentry's voice!

"Hi, dear. Not very good news, I'm afraid." The words came slowly, with long pauses in between. "I called the hospital at noon, and Dr. Osgood thinks it will be another two weeks. Timmy's getting better, but they have to clear up the infection before they dare let him come home."

Mrs. Gentry's voice trembled, then broke. "And John—some other things happened today. My stu-

16

dents were—well, I guess they couldn't know how much I needed to feel good about something today. No. No, I'll tell you about it tonight."

There was a long pause. Laurie's eyes blurred.

"Well, no, Dad won't be able to stay with the baby tonight, dear. We'll just have to take turns visiting the hospital. Hiring sitters for that long would cost too much. OK, John, I'll try to get away soon."

Laurie hurried out to her bus. The permission slip would have to wait. She didn't want Mrs. Gentry to see her.

If she was quieter than usual at the dinner table, Laurie's family didn't seem to notice. They didn't even notice that she went up to bed early, without saying good-night. She lay in the darkness, her body rigid, her mind whirling.

Teachers gave assignments. Teachers called roll and handed back theme papers and wrote page numbers on the chalkboard. But until right now she hadn't thought about teachers having money troubles and kids who got sick. Teachers were like everybody else. Sometimes they were worried and tired and their feelings were hurt.

"Help me, God," Laurie whispered. "I know it was wrong to do what the others did. Please show me how to make it right. Lord, I don't even know Mrs. Gentry's little boy, but please make him better."

The prayer just hung there, waiting for her "Amen." Then suddenly Laurie had her answer. If a whole class could be organized enough to walk right out of the building without getting caught, why

18

couldn't they be organized to help somebody with a problem? There had to be a way.

Well, all the girls she knew did some baby-sitting. Some of the boys, too. Maybe she could organize an emergency free sitting service for Mrs. Gentry's baby. She'd bring a chart to class tomorrow and ask everybody to sign up for a turn. Maybe some of them could sign up together. There could be an afternoon shift and an early evening shift.

Laurie scrambled out from under the covers and ran to call Julie and Melissa. When they heard about Timmy and about Mrs. Gentry's problem, they both agreed to help.

The next day Laurie walked to school so she could get there early. Long before time for science, Laurie had most of the time slots filled. At lunch there were just a few blank lines on the chart. Everybody seemed willing to help.

Laurie was more surprised than anybody when Andy Thompson got up from the table and came over to talk to her. "I hear you're lining up kids to help out with Mrs. Gentry's baby," he said. "Could I sign up?"

"Well," Laurie hesitated, "I guess so, but do you really think—?"

"I'm not all that bad a sitter," Andy sounded almost humble. "I've got two little sisters, and my mom works full time. And besides," he added with a sheepish smile, "this is Mrs. Gentry. I guess maybe I owe her."

19

"Sensible people will see trouble coming and avoid it, but an unthinking person will walk right into it and regret it later."

Proverbs 27:12 TEV

Tell me, God, why is it so easy to play Follow the Leader? Even when I know other kids will just get me into trouble, I fall right into step instead of doing what I know is right. Give me enough sense to make up my own mind. Amen.

Knowing Your Own Size

Mother doesn't fuss at me anymore about some things, like "Look out for cars" or "Did you remember to say thank you?" But she still thinks I can't take care of myself. How can I make her see I'm not a baby anymore?

For Wendy and her mother, the problem was school clothes. Shopping for clothes dug up all Wendy's feelings about being treated like a little kid.

"Honey," her mother said, "shouldn't I just go along so we'll be sure the clothes are something we both like, and that they fit properly and are practical?"

Wendy knew her mother was trying to be nice, but this time she had decided to stand her ground. "Mom, I'm not a baby anymore. I can take care of myself. I know what'll happen. Something will be the wrong color, and something else will wear out, and you won't think anything fits right. It's my Christmas money, and for once I want to pick out my own things. OK?"

Her mother bit her lip, looked down at the floor, then shrugged. "OK, Wendy, maybe you're right." She glanced at the clock. "There'll be a bus in about 10 minutes."

Wendy stood outside Mullenmeister's shoe store, studying the window display. Her eyes lingered on the ones with bouncy rubber soles and side buckles. Did she have enough money left, after buying the corduroy jacket and knee-highs? She strode through the big glass doors.

"May I help you?" The young man at the cash register came from behind the counter smiling.

"There's a pair of shoes in the window I'd like to try on." She pointed out the shoes in the display, then sat down in one of the yellow plastic chairs.

"Your foot measures size 6, but I think maybe 5½ will do it. This style runs large," he said cheerfully. He disappeared among the stacks of boxes, then came out with the shoes. He set the shoehorn back of her heel and twisted the shoe onto her foot.

She walked toward the tall mirror. Weren't they neat? Corky Henning had a pair a lot like them. She tried to wiggle her toes. They felt a little crowded, but new shoes always squeeze a little. Wendy was sure that when she'd worn them awhile they'd feel more comfortable. She had just enough money left to pay for them and still pay her bus fare home.

"Would you like to try on the other shoe?" the clerk offered.

"Oh, no, no, I just love them. I'm sure they'll be perfect."

Wendy hurried into the house and dumped everything out of the packages, watching for her mother's approval.

"Looks fine, Wendy. Did you feel grown up?"

"Oh, yes, I loved it."

Coming home from school the next day, Wendy seemed to be limping a little. She went to her room and reappeared wearing her slippers. Her mother looked at her thoughtfully, then went back to peeling potatoes.

Wendy mixed up some lemonade and sat down for a snack. Leaning both elbows on the table, cupping her chin in both hands, she said soberly, "Thanks, Mother, for not saying it."

"For not saying what?"

Wendy sighed. "For not saying 'I told you so.'"

"Shoes hurt, Wendy?" Mom asked gently.

"Yeah," she admitted, frowning. "Mom, I guess I really blew it. But I really did feel ready to shop for myself."

"And now you don't think you were ready?"

"Well, doesn't it look that way?"

Her mother ran water over the potatoes and set the kettle on the stove. She chose her words carefully. "Don't be too hard on yourself, Wendy. I don't agree with you. You are ready to shop. Look what a great-looking jacket you bought, and it fits just fine."

"Oh, sure, but what about the shoes?"

"You're ready to shop when you're ready to learn from your mistakes."

"What do you mean, Mom?"

"Wendy, I'd hate to tell you how many mistakes we made when we shopped for our first house. That sloping driveway didn't seem too bad, until winter came. In icy weather we couldn't even get the car into the garage. And I guess it was Dad who forgot to check for signs of water in the basement. We really did a dumb thing, buying that house. Well, we lived with those mistakes for six years, and we'll never make the same ones again."

"You mean that every time I want a pair of shoes that aren't exactly my size I'll remember these blisters?"

"Of course. And there's no way I can get your blisters for you. It's only your own experiences that help you grow up. You really are ready for new responsibilities. But Dad and I can be a sort of backup when something comes along that you can't handle quite yet."

"Maybe it's like when I switched from my trike to my bike. Training wheels saved me some bumps until I got used to it."

"Sure. Or like knitting. You're pretty good at it now, but you don't mind coming to me for emergency help when you've dropped a stitch."

"Remember that Bible story about the Pharisee who bragged about himself in church?" Wendy asked. "He thought he was bigger than everybody else, didn't he?"

"Yes. Jesus had a way of showing people what size they really were. Sometimes he actually had to cut them down to size. But you know God often tells us that we're bigger than we think we are. He promises to stand by while we try a really big job. Like when he made the young shepherd boy, David, feel big enough to face the giant, Goliath."

Wendy smiled. "Maybe we would never have heard about David if God hadn't moved him up to a bigger size."

"True, Wendy. And when Jeremiah felt too young to be God's prophet, God told him not to be afraid. He'd be there."

Wendy stuffed a cookie into her mouth. "Mom, I think you and my blisters have taught me something. Maybe some day I'll be really grown up like you are. Then I won't need to run to anybody for help."

Her mother laughed out loud. "Me? So grown up I don't need help? Wendy, if I ever get to feeling I'm so big I don't need anybody else, I'm in trouble. You still need me for some things, but do you know how much I need you? Let's both keep on trying to know our own sizes. Then we can be a lot of help to each other."

"But the Lord said to me, 'Do not say that you are too young, but go to the people I send you to, and tell them everything I command you to say. Do not be afraid of them, for I will be with you to protect you. I, the Lord, have spoken!'"

Jeremiah 1:7-8 TEV

I don't always know my own size, God. Sometimes I feel too big to need anybody else. Other times I feel too small to do anything. Match me up with jobs that fit me right now and jobs that give me a little growing room. Amen.

Kicking Out of the Cocoon

I really want to stay just the age I am now, but I know I can't. How can I feel better about it?

Kim sat quietly in her tree house, going through the things in a little wooden box. On the cover of the box she had burned the words: "Stuff for Remembering."

Kim looked at picture postcards from vacation trips and snapshots from Bible camp. There were shells from the shore and stubs from the Children's Theatre Christmas play. She turned over a piece of agate, then polished it with her shirttail.

Her eyes stung as she gazed out over the rooftops. She liked to be in the tree house when she had troubles.

Lately it felt like everybody in the world was tugging at her, trying to make her grow up before she felt ready, and Cindy was getting to be as bad as the rest.

When the other girls started polishing their nails and using lip gloss and talking about boys, at least she had always had Cindy. Cindy was always around to play Queen Bee or to wade across Wilson's Creek for a picnic. Now Cindy was changing, too. She actually seemed proud that her body was changing shape while Kim was still as flat as a paper doll.

Her parents were just as bad. "Act your age, Kim. You know, you're growing up." Pretty soon they'd even want to take the tree house down.

Grow up—grow up. They could all have it. Maybe Mom and Dad thought being grown-up was fun, but to her it was boring—sitting around talking about things like diets and septic tanks and committee meetings. Boring, boring, boring.

Kim piled the stuff back in the box and slid it under the bench.

"Guess I'll walk down to Grandma and Grandpa's," she thought. "Maybe Grandma baked coffee cake."

She backed down the ladder—strips of wood nailed to the tree trunk—then headed down the shaded street.

"Grandma, you home?" she called in through the screen door.

It was Grandpa's voice answering. "Kim, you came at just the right time! Come back to the kitchen."

He was sitting by the heavy oak table, peering into the side of a big peanut butter jar.

28

"Remember those pale green eggs we found on the milkweed plants?" he asked, not even looking up.

"Sure, Monarch butterfly eggs. And I was with you when we found those striped caterpillars that hatched from them."

"We put them in this jar with some sticks and leaves and then poked air holes in the cover. Well, they've been entertaining me ever since."

"Guess maybe I've missed part of the show, huh, Grandpa?"

"Well, you did miss Act Two, when the caterpillar made this cocoon."

Kim looked over Grandpa's shoulder at the little bullet-like object hanging from the roof of the jar.

"How come it's bluish? Last year the cocoons were light green."

"This one was, too, but this morning it's changing color. That means this is the big day—today we'll have a butterfly!"

"How can it just hang there from the jar cover?" Kim wondered.

"Well, that little striped caterpillar just crawled up there along the sticks and spun a sort of fine cable of threads. Then it hung there for a while just like a big J from your old alphabet book. Later the skin began to split off from the bottom of the J, and what a commotion that was!"

"Commotion?" Kim looked puzzled.

"Sure. That little thing swings around in a big, wild circle, getting rid of its striped skin. The skin gradually gets pushed up until it finally drops off in a little black wad. Then the caterpillar just pulls itself together into a sort of green pouch with a gold line around it, and you've got a cocoon."

"Look, Grandpa. It was bluish when I came. Now it's turning purple."

"Right. And you can begin to see through the covering. See that network of dark lines and those little spots? We're beginning to see the wings."

Kim was excited. "Ohhh, it's really a miracle, isn't it?" she whispered.

Now the cocoon was transparent and almost black. From under the gold line, long, jointed legs burst out, kicking awkwardly in all directions. A thin, clear husk, like cellophane, dropped to the bottom of the jar. Kim could tell it was a butterfly, but it still looked a little droopy. The body was fat and the wings were crumpled. The creature kept kicking, pumping fluid from its body into the wings. As the wings became stiffer and stronger, Kim could see the fine coloring of the Monarch—soft orange with a pattern of bold black lines and white dots at the wing tips.

"How's that for a beauty?" Grandpa asked, putting out a finger to form a perch. The long-legged butterfly clung to his finger.

Kim shook her head. "It wasn't exactly what I expected—all that wild kicking. I guess I thought a butterfly just sort of floated out of a cocoon like a ballet dancer coming out on stage."

"It isn't easy, Kim, leaving a part of yourself behind. It's tough, going from one stage to another, changing into something different. The caterpillar really had a time forming its cocoon, and you saw this morning how hard it was, leaving it. But now that the struggle's over, the butterfly is stronger and more beautiful than it's ever been. All of this was necessary to get the Monarch ready for bigger things. When those wings are completely dry, it'll be all set to fly clear down to Mexico."

"Mexico?"

"Right. They migrate all the way down to Mexico. Isn't that something?"

"You really love this, don't you, Grandpa?"

He nodded. "You can learn things from these creatures, Kim. That Monarch reminds me that to live means to change. Staying the same is a kind of death. It's a struggle for us, too, leaving childhood or young adulthood behind, but every stage in life can be just as interesting as the last."

He paused, then added, "I like to think God probably built something right into that little striped caterpillar that said, 'Hey, look, there's a lot more. Don't hold back in that cocoon. There's a whole world to see.'"

Kim sat silently for a while, just thinking. She swallowed hard before she spoke. "I guess I needed the butterfly today, Grandpa. I've been fighting with myself about growing up, sort of like that Monarch kicking its way into the next stage."

"I know how it is, Kim. Every stage of my life has been a little scary until I really got into it. Then it proved to be interesting. I've discovered it's not even too bad, growing old."

"I've always thought that would be terrible, Grandpa, but you seem to be doing OK."

"Well, if you can manage to keep growing, the 'good old days' can always mean right now. Take retirement. You know, I've loved these Monarchs for years, but I was always so busy running the feed store that I couldn't pay too much attention. Now I can get in on the going-away party before they take off for Mexico."

"That's neat. I'm glad I got in on it, too." Kim smiled, then reflected, "Being a kid is nice. I feel safe just where I am now, but I know that pretty soon I'll have to kick my way out of my cocoon."

Grandpa went to the counter and took the plastic cover off the coffee cake. He said quietly. "Yes, and you'll do just fine Kim. You'll do fine."

> "I know that there is nothing better for them than to be happy and enjoy themselves as long as they live."
>
> Ecclesiastes 3:12

Thank you, Lord, for growth, for all the changes that make life interesting. Thank you, too, for things that will never really change—things like home and friends and God. Amen.

Just a Little Lie

I'd never tell a really bad lie, but sometimes I change the facts a little just to make things easier for myself. Is that so serious?

"No, Mom, I haven't seen the candy dish." Casey glanced up, then quickly shifted her attention back to the music rack and lifted the clarinet to her mouth. It was hard to look at her mother when she said it, but it would have been harder still to admit that she had dropped the dish in the sink and then hidden the broken pieces under a layer of trash in the basket.

Was it so bad to stretch the truth a little? Her parents did it themselves sometimes. She had heard her mother say more than once, "I've got a lot to do at home today. Guess I'll call in sick at the office."

34

And Casey could still hear Dad tell that police officer that he had already arranged to have his noisy muffler fixed. Casey knew that just wasn't so, and she was surprised to hear Dad saying it.

If her parents stretched the truth, maybe she didn't need to worry too much about what she had learned in church school. The Bible probably meant serious lies, really important ones.

Her mother seemed to believe her story about the candy dish, so that lie worked out OK, and somehow the next one slid out a lot more easily. Pretty soon small lies were sprouting like dandelions. "It's OK with Tammy's mother if we go to the beach," she would say, or "I finished everything in school. I don't have any homework."

What harm was there in little fibs? They blocked off a lot of tiresome arguments. Mom never would have let her go to the shopping center today. That's why Casey had to say she was going to Nancy's to study.

"Mom keeps telling me she doesn't want me hanging around out here all the time," she told Nancy as they walked into the big central court. "You'd think I was going out here to have my ears pierced or something."

"Yeah," Nancy agreed. "My mom always thinks I come out here to mess around. It's just kind of neat to walk around looking at things. I told her I had to go to the library this afternoon. She'll never know."

They stood on the broad white steps and watched

35

foaming fingers of water spurting up from the fountain. Shoppers sat on backless benches munching on sandwiches or poking long spoons into milk-shake cups.

"Let's go to the upper level first," Nancy suggested. They hiked up the moving escalator, too impatient simply to let it carry them along.

Spicy, blossomy smells invited them into the This'n That Shop. Candles glowed in fat pots or shimmered from tall holders. They inspected cork bulletin boards and eggs enameled with blue flowers. Ladybug magnets clung to a metal display board.

"What if my mother calls your house?" Casey asked uneasily.

Nancy cut her off. "Stop that, Casey. I guess I should buy you some worry beads."

At Toy Town marionettes hung by their strings from the ceiling—Mickey Mouse and Pinocchio and Sleeping Beauty.

"Remember how we used to serve cookies from those dinky little tea sets?" Casey asked, feeling much too old for anything like that.

Nancy nodded. "The stuff in here is mostly for little kids, but I'd like that stuffed lion for my bed."

They walked by the elegant windows of the jewelry shop, where necklaces lay in their velvet-lined boxes. Hearing music, they stopped in the record shop. A singer clutching her guitar stared solemnly from the album cover on the Super Special display. The girls flipped through the used albums, but bought nothing.

They ignored the doorway of the Penny Arcade, where you could pose for a strip of photos or play the pinball machines. "I'm saving my money for something to eat," Casey announced. "You hungry yet?"

"I really should buy a card for Mother's Day. C'mon."

Just inside the door of the card shop, Casey froze in her tracks. "Quick, Nancy. Duck." She pulled her over behind the rack of gift wrap.

"What are you dragging me back here for, Casey?"

"Shhh. Our neighbor, Mrs. Tenney, is in there. I don't want her to see us and tell my mother."

"She's choosing paper plates," Nancy reported, poking her head around the corner of the rack. "Let's get out of here."

Safely back in the central court, they made their way to the Snack Station. "At home I can just squirt catsup or mustard on my hot dog, but here they have raw onions or honey sauce or Taco relish," Casey said, studying the overhead sign.

"How about all the ice cream flavors?" Nancy added. I think I'll try caramel almond crunch or whipped pineapple—maybe even licorice.

"Oh, no!" Casey groaned, grabbing her nose at the thought of licorice ice cream.

"We'd better eat something quick. They'll wonder about us at home," Nancy said.

A little later when Casey got home she found Dad at the telephone. Her mother, standing at his elbow, was dabbing at her eyes with a wet tissue.

Seeing Casey, Dad slammed the phone back on the hook and demanded in a loud voice, "Casey Cunningham, where have you been?"

"Just at Nancy's. I told Mom—"

"No, not at Nancy's." He spoke in a cold, level voice. "You were never at Nancy's. The Bradleys stopped by to invite you to ride along to the amusement park, and—"

"I missed going to Fun Fair? Ohhhh, no!"

"Oh, yes. We called Nancy's house, and they said no, you hadn't been around and Nancy was at the library. Then we really got worried."

"Casey, I've been half out of my mind," her mother said, "worried that something terrible had happened to you. We were just going to call the police."

"All right, I was at the shopping center. I didn't mean to worry you, Mom. I just planned to be back so soon that I thought it would be OK. I guess I thought you wouldn't find out."

"And maybe we wouldn't have if the Bradleys hadn't come." Mom paused. "You thought we'd never know, but, Casey, you would know. Isn't that important to you?"

"Lately I've tried to tell myself that little lies aren't serious," Casey admitted, "but after I tell any lie I still feel uncomfortable. Why is that?"

"I guess that means you're lucky enough to have a tender conscience," Dad answered.

"Lucky? It feels terrible."

"But lucky, honey. That conscience is God's yellow

38

caution light. It slows you down a little, but it might save your life."

"Don't get mad if I tell you this, but you both lie sometimes, too," Casey ventured timidly.

"You mean we've lied to you, Casey?" Dad sounded puzzled.

"Well, not so much to me, but I heard you lie to the policeman about that muffler. And Mother sometimes calls in sick when she isn't sick at all."

There was a long silence while her parents digested Casey's words. They looked uncomfortable, and Casey wished she could take back what she had said. Dad didn't get mad. He just nodded thoughtfully and said, "I guess you're right. We all do it." Then he added. "But why? Maybe that's important. Why do we lie?"

Casey said she wasn't sure.

"Well, I think I lied to that police officer because I was afraid," Dad went on, "afraid I'd get a ticket and have to pay a fine."

"And I suppose I lied about being sick because I was afraid, too—afraid of what the boss might say if I just asked for a day off," Mom said.

Casey was beginning to understand. "I guess I lied about the shopping center because I was afraid, too. I thought I'd be punished for going there."

"Now that I think about it," Mom said, "I guess it really hasn't always paid for you to tell the truth, Casey. I've punished you or scolded you when you've admitted doing something wrong, so maybe lying seemed an easier way out."

Dad summed it up, "Well, I guess we all tell lies because we're afraid of what will happen if people know the truth."

"But today I found out that bad things can also happen when people don't know the truth. I missed out on going to Fun Fair, and I made Mom cry."

"Yes, it isn't every day you miss out on a trip to the amusement park, but every lie does have consequences. The important thing is, what do we do about all of this?"

"Let's make a pact that from now on the truth will be honored in this house," Casey's mother said. "Let's not be afraid to talk things over, to work things out. Maybe if we had talked over this shopping center trip we could have worked out a way for you to go there without being a bother to people in the stores."

"Sounds good," Dad agreed. "We're a family. We love each other. Why should we lie out of fear? Families should be able to count on each other. Right, Casey?"

Casey grinned. "Right."

> "A lie has a short life, but truth lives on forever."
>
> Proverbs 12:19 TEV

I can see it now, Lord. Lies aren't necessary to people who love each other. Make me uncomfortable when I have been careless with the truth. Amen.

I Feel Sorry for Her

I feel sorry for a girl in my school who has to go everywhere in a wheelchair. I know I should be friendly to her, but I don't know how to act.

Molly was in a hurry, so she threw her books up on her locker shelf, grabbed her jacket, and slammed the metal door. Almost running through the crowded corridor, she thrust a hand through one sleeve and pulled the jacket around her. She started to zip it up with a mighty yank. Stuck! Just inches from the bottom, the zipper was frozen in place. Molly groaned.

Then she heard a voice. "Need some help?"

Jerking her head around, she looked back over her shoulder. She was surprised to see Kerry Benson. Molly had seen Kerry around school. You couldn't help noticing her scooting through the halls in her wheelchair. Somewhere Molly had heard that Kerry had been born with "open spine," and that she had something called a shunt, a little pump under her scalp that pumped fluid out of her brain and down through a tube into her heart. That sounded scary.

Molly had helped Kerry a couple of times in the cafeteria, carrying her tray over to a table, but she had never thought about Kerry being able to help anybody else.

"I'm pretty good at zippers," Kerry offered. "Why don't you let me try?"

Well, why not? Molly was too upset to work at it herself.

She took off the jacket, piled it on Kerry's lap, and watched her clever fingers go to work. Kerry gave the zipper a little twist, pulling away the cloth that had become entangled in the teeth. She slid the tab down a little, then moved it smoothly to the top.

That was the beginning of their friendship. At first they just said hi, then talked a little between classes. When Kerry found out that Molly was interested in weaving, she asked her to come over after school to see some of her things.

Molly looked in silent admiration at the handsome book bag Kerry had woven to hang on her wheelchair. Suddenly her own little belts and wall hangings seemed a little shabby. When Kerry offered to get her started weaving a Christmas table runner, Molly became a regular visitor at the Benson home.

Until then the only disabled kids Molly had known were characters in books. They seemed to spend

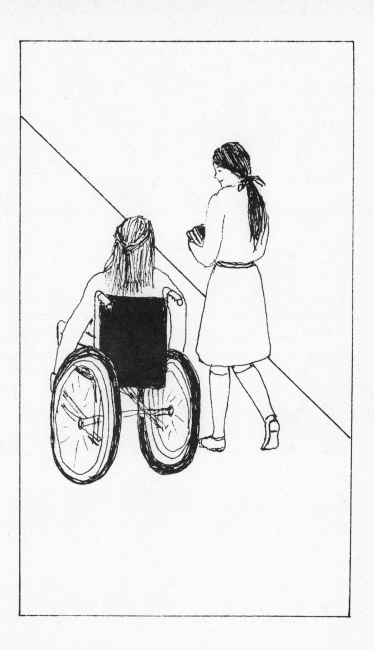

most of their time sitting by a window watching the other kids play, smiling bravely to hide their loneliness. They spoke softly about noble things.

Kerry wasn't anything like that. Her laugh was loud, and she was always busy, playing her guitar or tooling leather or weaving. Her parents didn't baby her, either. She put away a lot of her own things, and she had to load the dishwasher and sweep floors and sharpen her dad's tools.

Molly was almost relieved to find out that Kerry wasn't as noble as those kids in the books she'd read. Kerry was far from perfect. She got into fights with her brother, and sometimes she sneaked cake before dinner.

Molly discovered that the Bensons had to plan ahead more than most families. Before they went to any house or store, they had to check in advance to find out if there would be steps to climb and whether bathroom doors would be wide enough for a wheelchair. Snow meant trouble, because it might clog the spokes in the wheels.

Molly invited Kerry to join her Girl Scout troop, and they went swimming together.

One night Kerry went with Molly and her dad to a high school basketball game. Molly's dad worried a little about managing the wheelchair, but it worked out fine. Kerry just wheeled up to the side of the car, removed the left arm from the chair, supported herself with her hands as she slid onto the car seat, then used her hands to lift one leg at a time into the car.

44

After the game, Kerry had an idea. "Molly, how would you like to come with me to the Rehab Center next Saturday? The Rolling Sharpshooters have a morning game. I'm planning to try out for the team myself after I've had a little more therapy."

Hey, neat! Molly's first chance to watch wheelchair basketball.

It was a game she would never forget. The warm-up was almost like a parade, with each player in turn rolling under the basket for a lay-up shot. Then each team wheeled into a circle, piled hands together, and shouted, "Let's go!" Wheelchairs glided to their positions.

In some ways it was like any basketball game, with most of the same rules. In other ways it was like no game Molly had ever seen. A player would stroke a wheel with one hand while dribbling or passing with the other. Then she would set the ball on her lap, slap at the wheels with both hands as she raced down the floor, then swivel sharply and go off in another direction. Traveling was legal, and these girls really traveled in style.

At first Molly couldn't take her eyes off of their feet. Some wore brown loafers, and others, tennis shoes or boots. From some shoes, metal braces went up the leg under the sweat pants. One player had a sole three inches thick, while another had only a folded-over pants leg where her foot should have been.

But after a while, feet seemed unimportant. Molly

45

saw only strong arms stretching high for a pass or strong shoulders pushing off a long shot.

The man who passed out the water bottles during time-out also brought a screwdriver and a wrench, in case a wheelchair needed a quick repair.

"Gets rough, doesn't it?" Kerry asked with a grin as the players chased a ball the length of the court. A fast break was a frantic chariot race with chairs clanking together, then stalling in a wild traffic jam.

A girl with feet as limp as a rag doll's fell off her chair. The crowd grew quiet, but nobody made a move to help her. She crawled and stretched and struggled, finally hoisting herself up on the seat and wheeling back into play.

Molly was worried, but Kerry said, "She doesn't need help." The players were like Kerry. They wanted to do things for themselves.

When the game was over, Molly went along to Kerry's therapy group. She watched Kerry doing "push-ups," pushing with her hands to raise herself from the chair, then slowly lowering herself to the seat, again and again.

"Hi," said a voice beside Molly. The husky man with the red beard was talking to her. "I'm Brad, the therapist," the man said. "You're Kerry's friend, aren't you?"

"Yes, I'm Molly."

Kerry lay on a table with weights on her legs. Brad explained, "Kerry has to spend time in traction so the muscles don't draw together under her knees."

"Rehab Center is really a great place," said Molly.

"I noticed handrails in all the halls and automatic sliding doors. Drinking fountains and elevator buttons are low enough so kids like Kerry can reach them from a wheelchair."

"All public buildings should be built with wheelchair ramps and wide doors and roomy bathrooms. It's the only way disabled people will be able to go out and take a job. They don't ask for special favors, but they'd like an even break."

Molly confided: "You may not believe this, but I used to be kind of afraid of Kerry."

Brad nodded. "I'm not surprised. Maybe way deep down you're a little afraid it could happen to you. I'll bet you used to think Kerry was really different from you."

"We're a lot alike. We both like pizza and weaving and swimming. She can't do everything, but I can't do everything either."

"Molly, were you ever in a sack race where you had to run with your feet and legs tied in a gunnysack? It was fun for a while because you knew that soon you could take off the sack, but it wouldn't be fun for a lifetime. In rehabilitation we have to get these kids ready for a lifetime like that."

"Yeah, doing everything the hard way."

"Kerry's legs are damaged, but here she learns new ways of doing things so she isn't handicapped in any important way. She's got to grow up whole inside. Kerry has good hands. She doesn't need a new way to feed herself or draw pictures, but if her hands didn't work we'd teach her to paint pictures holding a brush in her teeth."

"You know, if I had Kerry's problems I might blame God for making some terrible mistake when I was born," Molly said soberly. "Kerry doesn't see it that way. She says God has given her a lot of skills. She's so good at things that it's hard to feel sorry for her."

"Kerry doesn't need your pity, but she can use your friendship. We can do a lot for her here, but I can't be an ablebodied friend her own age. You can."

> "But he said to me, 'My grace is sufficient for you, for my power is made perfect in weakness.'"
>
> 2 Corinthians 12:9

Everybody's weak in some ways, Lord. I am, too. Teach me how to be friends with everyone, looking for what is strong in each person. Amen.

I Keep Hoping

My mother and dad are divorced, but I'm still hoping they'll get back together again. If I show them how much it means to me, do you suppose they'll change their minds?

Emmy tied the long paper dress at the back of her neck and sat down. Why hadn't she brought a magazine along from the waiting room? There was nothing to do until the doctor came in. She looked out the little window, but there wasn't much to see, only a brick wall and a pile of gray clouds sliding across the sky.

"I hope he doesn't decide to give me a shot," she thought, seeing the rows of bottles and a big jar of cotton balls lined up neatly on the cabinet.

How about those wooden things, like popsicle

sticks? Maybe if she could poke one back on her tongue like Dr. Kellogg did, she'd be able to throw up. She'd better decide what disease she had before he got there. A ruptured appendix, maybe. Which side was the pain supposed to be on? Did appendicitis make you throw up?

Maybe just plain pain would be easier to pretend. She hadn't really told her mother what was wrong, only that she felt awfully sick, sick enough for the hospital.

The examination went OK. Holding his fingers flat, Dr. Kellogg pressed down first on one place, then another.

"How does that feel, Emmy?" he asked, pressing on her left side. Emmy flinched. She tried to remember how she had felt that time after she'd eaten a party-size pizza all by herself. She squeezed her eyes shut, gasping in a little air, holding her breath for a second, then letting it out with a long sigh.

"That hurt quite a lot," "she reported sadly, her voice trembling. "Do you suppose it's appendicitis?"

"Well, Emmy, you don't have a temperature, and your color is good. From what I've seen I can't really diagnose what's wrong, but if your pain is that severe maybe we'd better put you into the hospital overnight and do some tests.

A smile flickered across Emmy's face, but she quickly hid it under an agonized expression. The hospital! She was going to the hospital! Her plan was working. Now if only Dad would come home to Poplar City.

An hour later she was lying in a hospital bed. As her mother turned the crank, she could feel the shifting mattress bending in the middle and pushing against her shoulders until she was sitting halfway up. It felt good.

"Get some rest now, honey. Everything's going to be all right," Mom said. "I'll come here first thing in the morning." Her mother brushed her forehead with a kiss and tiptoed from the room.

For the first time since her parents told her about the divorce, Emmy dared to let herself hope. She forced herself to remember all the events that had brought her here. It would have been easy to leave out the bad parts—like how much it used to hurt to hear them fighting.

"I don't appreciate your getting home so late," her mother would say.

"Well, maybe I don't appreciate your nagging when I get here," her dad would answer.

Their fighting never seemed to be about important things. When Emmy came around they would sometimes shut the door or suddenly quit talking. Finally, the battles tapered off and things got quiet—too quiet.

That silence had puzzled her. If they weren't mad anymore, why didn't they ever kiss like they used to? It was like they didn't even see each other. Dad would work late and Mom would run off to gourmet cooking class, only she never fixed any of the recipes at home. Or Mom would stare at a book while Dad sat playing solitaire, slapping cards down on the table, getting angry when he lost. Emmy started going to Kelly's house a lot so she wouldn't have to think about it.

She'd never forget the day they told her. There was chicken for dinner, but nobody ate much. Mom was crying and Dad looked bleak and anxious. Emmy felt crushed under a load of sorrow and anger and shame.

"We're sad because it's hard for you, Emmy," Mom had said, "but living together has become too painful. Maybe if we're in separate places we can someday become friends again."

In the following months, Emmy had tried everything to make them start over. She tried making up stories, telling her father that her mother missed him a lot, or the other way around. But nothing happened.

Once she pleaded so hard that Dad actually moved back in for a few days, but Mom got so gloomy and Dad got so edgy that soon he packed up and left again.

And Emmy prayed. Over and over she begged God to make things right. Even God didn't seem to care.

But now, maybe this time. . . .

She pictured both of them beside her bed, sick with worry. Mom would lean against Dad for strength. He would put a comforting arm around her shoulder, and suddenly they would be in each other's arms, swept together by rediscovered love. Emmy closed her eyes and sighed. It could work. It *had* to work.

Suddenly she felt hungry. She had convinced both

her mother and Dr. Kellogg that she couldn't eat a bite, but she had lied.

Emmy looked over at her roommate to make sure she was sleeping. Then she slipped into her robe, fished some coins out of the drawer beside her bed, and sneaked out of the room.

Nobody was sitting in the lounge as Emmy walked up to the sandwich machine and studied the pictures. Deciding that the ham and cheese looked more interesting than the roast beef or the turkey, she slid coins into the slot, then grabbed the ham and cheese handle.

"Why, Emmy, you were hungry after all."

Her fingers froze to the handle. She wanted to run, run anywhere, but she just stood there, looking at Dr. Kellogg.

"This is a good place to talk, Emmy. Go ahead and pick up your ham and cheese. Then why don't we sit down here a minute?"

They sat down on the blue sofa.

"There's no use talking, Dr. Kellogg. You've found out now."

"I've found out?'"

"That there's nothing wrong with me, that I don't have appendicitis or anything."

"I know you don't have appendicitis, Emmy. I knew that back in my office, but I can't agree that there's nothing wrong. There's always something wrong when a girl decides she wants to be sick. I'd like to help you with whatever it is."

"Nothing can help now, Dr. Kellogg," she sighed.

"I know I shouldn't take a room that's for people who are really sick, but could I stay for just a few more hours?"

"Do you like hospitals that much?"

"Well, I did want both Mom and Dad to come here. It's important."

"Is it the divorce, Emmy?" Dr. Kellogg's voice was soft and gentle, and she wasn't afraid of him anymore.

"All I want is for all of us to be together and happy again."

"When you were all together, were you really happy? Now be honest with yourself, Emmy."

She admitted to him how miserable she had felt during the fights. "But it wasn't any better when the shouting stopped. It was like all the angry words they used to say were bubbling around inside of them, and sometime the cork was bound to pop." Emmy looked down at her feet. "I guess I shouldn't be telling you all this."

"Don't deny your feelings, Emmy. It's good for you to talk about it."

"Sometimes I would worry that it was my fault. Even after the divorce I used to try to be very good so they would remarry."

"They didn't divorce because you were bad, Emmy, but because they were unhappy."

"They both told me that they weren't divorcing me. They stopped loving each other, but they didn't stop loving me. Just the same, I'd like to help them."

"And you can, Emmy. You've wanted to help your

parents by putting their marriage back together again, but there are other ways you can help."

"Mother seems to need me now."

"You bet she does. You can help her take care of things around the house. You can be somebody for her to talk to in her loneliness, too, but don't try to be a grown-up. She needs you as her daughter, not as a substitute for your dad."

"I prayed about it, Dr. Kellogg, but I don't think God was listening."

"Praying is not like wishing on a star, Emmy. God listens to every prayer, but he isn't like a wizard granting everybody three wishes. God wants marriages to last, but mostly he wants real happiness in a home."

"Do you mean God is telling me to give up?"

"He may be saying to you, 'Hand this problem over to me.' He wants us to care. He even invites us to pray that others will decide in the right way, but he gives people freedom to make their own choices. He doesn't force his will on anyone, and you can't force your will on your parents, either. This divorce isn't your problem, Emmy. It's theirs."

"It makes me sad. Doesn't that make it my problem?"

"If you just make the best of it and start over in another direction, your sadness will get better. But if you keep hoping, then there's no chance for God to heal your unhappy feelings. Your sadness and anger will just hang on. Remember, Emmy, all of you are in God's care. Try to leave the details up to him."

"I'll try, Dr. Kellogg. Do you suppose I'm well enough to go home?"

The doctor answered with a big wink. "That would be my professional diagnosis, Emmy. Suppose we call your mother and arrange it."

> "Your joy is your own; your bitterness is your own. No one can share them with you."
>
> Proverbs 14:10 TEV

Are you trying to tell me something, Lord? Help me to learn that I can't decide things for my parents, even when I think they're wrong. If you've decided not to change the way things are, help me handle my unhappiness, and help my parents find whatever happiness you have planned for them. Amen.

Work, Work, Work

All my mother wants me to do is work, work, work. Shouldn't a kid have some time just for fun?

Jill Krueger was a whiz in school and an athlete, too, with a volleyball serve as sharp as her math skills. She had friends, but she never asked any of them to her house after school. To tell the truth, she would have been ashamed.

Jill's mother was smart, and she was in charge of a lot of important committees, but she was a terrible housekeeper. It would have bothered Jill to have her friends see the papers strewn all over the dining room table, the litter of apple cores and orange peelings in the ashtrays, the unmade beds and overflowing trash cans.

Tina Randolph knew why Jill made excuses, and

she felt sorry for her. Often she'd invite Jill to go home with her from school. Tina knew that whenever friends walked through her front door, they would find a house in perfect order. The pajamas she had stepped out of in the morning would be neatly hung in the closet, and her bed would be made. Kitchen counters would be gleaming, towels would be hanging straight, wash bowls would be scrubbed. You could breathe in the clean smells of soap and furniture polish.

Tina and her friends were usually welcomed with a glass of milk and a warm cookie. If Tina had thought about it, she may have given her mother great marks for housekeeping, but Tina had never thought about it.

One day when Tina brought Jill home with her, the front door was locked.

"Mother must have gone to the store—or maybe collecting for cerebral palsy," Tina said, feeling for the key back of the planter.

The first thing she noticed in the hall was a note, taped neatly to the wall, addressed "To Bob and the children."

"Strange," thought Tina. "Since when does Mother leave notes?"

"Dear Family," she read. "I'll be at Grandpa's for a few days. I'm fine. I love you all. I'll explain later. Mother."

Gone? Her mother? What had gone wrong at Grandpa's? Why would she take off without even letting them know ahead of time? It was weird.

Only Mother's calm words, "I'm fine. I love you all," kept her from panic.

She called Dad at his law office, but he had no answers.

"Are you sure, Tina?"

"I'm sure."

"You mean she didn't even leave dinner in the oven?"

Tina reached over and switched on the oven light. "No, Dad. Nothing."

"Just sit tight and don't worry, Tina," he said. "I'll stop at the store on the way home and pick up some TV dinners and potato chips and cold cuts."

That night's dinner wasn't too bad. They read directions before heating up the aluminum trays with their neat piles of fried chicken and vegetables and apple dessert. The cooking wasn't like Mother's, and Mother would have given Kip a smaller helping of carrots, but it was interesting to taste a TV dinner.

Mother's phone call that night explained a few things. Grandpa had fallen and broken his ankle. When the doctor called, she had decided to go to Baytown to help Grandpa for a few days. Dad had been out of the office when she tried to reach him, and Donna Conroy next door had offered to take her to the airport.

The kids could hear Dad saying, "Well, I suppose you have a list of things for us to do to keep the household afloat till you get back?"

As he listened to her answer, a bewildered expression spread over his face. Finally, he said, "Well,

OK, Diana, I guess we'll manage somehow," and slowly he hung up.

"You look funny, Daddy," Annie said. "Is Grandpa awful sick?"

Dad sat down heavily and shook his head.

"Well, not sick, Annie, but he is in the hospital. He fell off a stepladder and broke his ankle." Dad paused. "I guess I'm more worried about your mother."

"Mom? Is she sick?"

"Well, I guess not, but she's . . . different."

"Different?"

"Yes. I asked her if she had a list of things for us to do till she got back."

"Yeah, we heard," Tina said. "Well, did she?"

"No. She said, 'I'm afraid not—you'll just have to play it by ear,' as if she didn't even care. Then she laughed and told me, 'It's a long story, Bob. Grandpa drew me a picture. I'll tell you about it when I see you.'"

Kip grinned. "Grandpa is always drawing neat pictures."

Tina looked stunned. "Yeah, but not magical ones. Who ever heard of drawing a picture that could change somebody into a different kind of person?"

Dad put on a tight little smile and tried to reassure them. "Well, kids, I was probably imagining things. I told her we'd manage, and we will. Soon she'll be back and everything will return to normal."

Somehow Bob Randolph and his children did manage, although a mountain of clothes grew under the laundry chute and a film of dust settled over everything. At first they filled up on cold cereal and sandwiches and frozen dinners. Then they got a little braver and tried other things. The spaghetti was glued together in one big lump, and the scrambled eggs were streaked with brown, but everybody was hungry, so they ate.

When the phone rang Saturday morning, Tina raced downstairs to answer it. "Tina? Hi!" It was good to hear Mother's voice.

"Listen, honey, I'll be landing at 1:30 today. That's Universal Airlines, Flight 25. Got that? OK, Tina. See you later."

Today! 1:30 today! Suddenly all Tina could see was clutter. Dirty dishes towered on the counters. Scraps of carrot peelings and cooked spaghetti clogged the sink strainers. Gritty little crumbs dug into the soles of her bare feet. What would Mother think?

"Dad, get up. Come on, you guys. We gotta shape up. Mother's coming home! She'll be here by 1:30."

Tina felt pretty stupid about where to begin, but soon the little kids were up on their feet, and Dad was barking orders.

"Kip, you go through the living room and family room and pick up every shoe you see. Tina, could you scrub the sink while I load the dishwasher? Annie, empty all the wastebaskets. Would somebody scrape the egg yolk off that burner? Get those toothpaste specks off the mirror. . . ."

How much could they get done before 1:30? Tina

61

rushed breathlessly from sink to bedroom to trash can.

"This is fun," she decided secretly. "Almost like playing Beat the Clock."

At 1:00 they all collapsed into the car and headed for the airport. "First thing Mother will do when she gets home will be to inspect the kitchen," Tina guessed. But, no, she strode straight through to the family room. "We've got to talk," Mother said.

"We do?" Kip scratched his head.

"Well, at least I do," she said briskly. "If I don't tell you this right away, I'm afraid I'll never say it."

Dad was right. Mother had changed.

Then she told them about the first afternoon in Baytown, sitting by Grandpa's bed. After a quick look at the cast encasing his ankle and a few cheery words like, "Hey, there, what are you trying to pull?" she began to sort nervously through her purse, pulling out scraps of paper and writing things down.

"All of the unfinished jobs I'd left back here when I'd rushed off to the airport kept poking at me," she recalled. "Would anybody notice that the plants needed water? The dust bag on the vacuum cleaner was probably full, and who would clean the litter-box? I had this terrible feeling I had abandoned you all. I think I actually prayed for your survival."

"Well, after about 10 minutes of this, Grandpa shook his head and asked for a pencil and paper. I felt one of his drawings coming on."

"What did he draw this time?" Kip wanted to know.

Diana Randolph
Slave Mother

"You remember when you kids were in kindergarten and had to draw pictures of your father and mother?" They nodded.

"Well, Grandpa sketched a beauty. There was this stick person in a ruffled apron with heavy chains around her ankles. Then in big scrawly letters he wrote the words 'Diana Randolph—Slave Mother.'"

"Slave Mother?" said Annie, wrinkling up her forehead. "I don't get it."

"Well, I think I do," Dad said. "All of us have just expected to come home every day to a perfect house. I guess we figured that a merry little band of elves trooped in while we were gone and whisked away the mess."

"Grandpa asked me, 'If a house isn't just so, why does everybody in town say it's the mother who's a bad housekeeper? If a whole family lives in a house, then a whole family should keep it clean.'"

"Maybe Grandpa's right," Tina agreed. "We've had one housekeeper trying to keep up with four house-messers."

"Well, he convinced me that I wasn't doing anybody a favor by raising three kids who don't even know how to scramble an egg."

And that's how Tina's lawyer father got the idea for drawing up an official Emancipation Proclamation for Slave Mothers. It was a pretty simple plan, with each of the kids agreeing to keep his or her own room clean. It also mapped out a plan for sharing chores in the areas they all used, like bathrooms and kitchen and family room.

Since then, there are some days when the kids complain about "work, work, work," but they enjoy seeing Mother more relaxed. And the whole family felt proud of her the day she went out and found a part-time job selling real estate. Tina's family found out the hard way how to share in keeping their house.

> "Whatever your task, work heartily, as serving the Lord and not men."
>
> Colossians 3:23

How come it takes me so long to figure things out, Lord? Is it because I'm thinking so hard about myself that I don't really look at my own family? Remind me that housekeeping is a job for all of us together. Amen.

Leftovers for God

Is it fair when my parents expect me to pay church dues out of my allowance? By the time I've bought lunches and school supplies and spent a little for Cokes and movies, I don't have anything left over for the church.

For a while Sarah tried to tune out the church-school discussion group. She was tired of hearing about giving money to church. Then she had a crazy impulse. "I'll try to remember my penny next week!" she said.

Pastor Gunderson joined in the laughter, but then he pulled his chair right up in front of Sarah and challenged her.

"Does a penny seem about right to you, Sarah?"

"Well," she answered with a shrug, "I've got to have some money left for fun."

"And it's no fun taking part in the offering, right?"

Fun? Sarah thought about the sober ceremony of offering time at church. She pictured the solemn man in the dark suit who stood beside the pew, his back to the altar. She could see him handing the brass plate to the person on the aisle, then quickly looking away, shoulders stiff, hands clasped behind his back, his face expressionless. As the plate passed from hand to hand each person silently fished something from purse or pocket and added it to the pile.

Fun? Offering time wasn't her idea of fun, but Pastor Gunderson was waiting for an answer. "Well, I suppose the church does need money," Sarah said lamely.

"Giving will never be fun for you unless you see what your money is doing."

Sarah snorted a half-laugh, embarrassed. "It's never that much money."

"Want to find out whether you get your money's worth?"

Sarah looked puzzled. "How would I do that?"

"Well, for openers, how would you like to hang around with me for a day?"

"Me? With you?"

"Sure. See what my day is like. As a church member, you're my boss. You should know what I'm up to. Tell you what. There's no school tomorrow. I'll stop by for you about 8:30. OK?"

Sarah agreed to that. She liked Pastor Gunderson.

He went to football games and played guitar, and you didn't need to look up his words in a dictionary.

Next morning when the blue station wagon pulled up in front of the farmhouse, Sarah gulped down her orange juice, kissed her mother, and hurried out the door. Bright sunlight warmed the wagon as they headed toward town. On both sides of the road, spring plowing had striped the fields with moist brown ridges.

As they came to the Jensen place, a big green tractor lumbered over the field in their direction. Pastor Gunderson slowed down and pulled off the road. "Joe Jensen has been wanting to talk to me."

He waved at the man in the cab. The tall farmer turned off the roaring motor, then climbed down and strode toward them. After shaking hands, Joe Jensen told Pastor Gunderson what was on his mind.

"It's about Gary," he said, pushing the visored cap back on his head. "The boy has been working hard with me ever since high school. I'd like to think he'll be farming here after I'm gone, but he shouldn't be just my hired hand until I'm an old man. I'd like to work something out so he could gradually gain an interest in the home place. But I want to be fair to the other kids, too."

"A father-son agreement," the pastor nodded. "These things can be worked out. It's important to you to keep the home place in family hands."

"That's right. Important to me and good for the community."

"And certainly for our church. We need the Jensens. Tell you what, Joe, I'll talk to Bill Ames about this. You'll need a lawyer. Then we can set up a meeting for you and Marge and all your kids."

"Good. I'd appreciate that. We'd all feel better if we had it settled."

"A country pastor has to think about the future of the land," Pastor Gunderson said as they drove away. "You farm families are important to us."

The phone was ringing as they walked into the pastor's book-lined office. "Hi, Bonnie." Pastor Gunderson smiled as he spoke. "How's the Good Neighbor committee doing on the Hanley project? Good. I'll put something in the bulletin. I'm sure some of the men will help get the crop in. Norm's doing pretty well, but he's got to take it easy."

As he hung up, he explained, "Norm Hanley hurt his hand in that combine accident last fall. We've been helping the family out until he's back at work."

The morning mail had come in. Pastor Gunderson ripped open a carton on his desk and handed Sarah a new book.

"Take a look. These are for the sixth-grade church school class."

"*Jesus and His Friends*. Looks pretty good."

"It is. But Sarah, you and I are paying $90 for this one box of books. The future of the church depends on how well we teach the children, but education costs money."

As he emptied a big envelope, the pastor asked, "What do you know about world hunger?"

"Well, we learned in school that it's really getting

to be a problem. Africa, South America—I forget all the places where people are starving."

"Your church is doing something about it. Take a look at this material."

Until she looked at those pamphlets, hunger hadn't seemed real to Sarah. But these people were really starving. She saw desperate hands stretching out for a skimpy bowl of rice. She saw hollow-eyed babies with bony arms, their abdomens bloated as round as a basketball.

Sarah was startled to read that a child in Bangladesh could be well fed for a few cents a day. "Wow! If I just stopped drinking Cokes I could help feed a starving child for a week," she thought.

She learned that the church wasn't only handing out bags of emergency food. It was sponsoring projects like bee-keeping and tree-planting and well-digging, so someday these people could produce more of their own food.

A brown-bag lunch in the church kitchen broke up the day for Pastor Gunderson and Sarah. Then they stopped by the Jasper home, where a moving van stood in the drive. The family felt sad about leaving Creston, but they were glad to know that Pastor Gunderson had written to a pastor in Apple City asking him to look them up.

At the hospital Sarah and her pastor walked from room to room visiting sick people. Some of them, smiling and comfortable, seemed to be just sleeping late. But some faces were twisted with pain. One man broke into sobs as the pastor prayed.

Sarah almost had to run up the curving drive at Restview Nursing Home to keep pace with the pastor. Sunlight poured in through the windows of the lounge, where old people sat on sofas or in wheelchairs, their legs covered by bright lap robes like Grandma's patchwork quilt.

Pastor Gunderson made the rounds, shaking hands, asking questions, sometimes nodding in sympathy, often laughing. They stopped by a long table where old men and women were dabbing glaze on ceramic vases and candy dishes and figurines.

"Remember Mrs. Werner?"

Sarah smiled. "I remember those lemon cakes she always brought to the harvest supper. Dad says she used to be his Sunday school teacher."

"Come with me to her room. She's asked for private communion."

They found her sitting by her window, sunlight resting on the silvered brown of her hair. Soft blue yarn unreeled from the fat ball in her basket to the needles in her hands. They talked for a while about church, news of the town, and Sarah's family. Mrs. Werner invited Sarah to come some time to play checkers.

"How old are you now, Sarah?"

"I'm 10—almost 11."

"That's a good age," Mrs. Werner chuckled softly. "I'll promise not to let you win, and you'll have to promise not to let me win. We'll really play checkers."

A hush fell over the room as Pastor Gunderson

read the holy words of the communion service from a thin red book. Mrs. Werner's hand, stiff and etched with blue veins, trembled as she reached for the glass. Her whole body seemed to say the prayers.

Leaving Restview, the pastor said, "I'll run you home now, Sarah. I have to go home for dinner before tonight's wedding rehearsal."

The yard light was already on and Dad was in from the fields as they pulled up to the farmhouse.

"Thanks, Pastor Gunderson. I think I'm getting my money's worth."

"Good. I thought a little show and tell would be be better than a sermon."

"It sure was. When my folks used to mention the offering, all I could see was coins. From now on I'll be able to see faces—Mrs. Werner's and Joe Jensen's and all those starving kids."

As she opened the door, she had another thought. "You know, Pastor, Dad might let me raise a calf and send the money to Bangladesh. I think I'd like that."

> "Each one must do as he has made up his mind, not reluctantly or under compulsion, for God loves a cheerful giver."
>
> 2 Corinthians 9:7

I admit it, Lord. I've been giving you the leftovers. Teach me to see real faces behind the collection plate. Amen.

I Dare You

When the other kids dare me to do something, I'm always chicken. How can I get over it?

Mrs. Potter looked at the back of her daughter's head, bowed quietly, a few pews ahead of her in church. "Meg seems to be behaving herself today," she thought proudly. "She isn't whispering and giggling like some of the others."

Her mother didn't know it, but Meg wasn't noticing the choir or the prayers or the organ music. She was too busy flipping through the bubble gum cards that Nicole had passed to her during the opening hymn. She paused, studying one card.

"Now there's one I don't have yet. I wonder if Nicole would—"

She was only half-listening to the voice from the

pulpit, but something seemed different. She glanced up. It wasn't Pastor Bernhoff. There was a visiting speaker, taller and younger than Pastor Bernhoff, and he was looking straight down at her class in the fourth pew.

"And if any of you kids have pictured Jesus as a pale, faraway figure who doesn't know about your feelings, I dare you to climb up to the top of the temple with him. I dare you to stand beside him when Satan advises him to jump off."

"I dare you!" Meg winced. The last time she had heard those words was Thursday afternoon. She was at the top of the hill on Mulberry Street. One foot rested on her orange skateboard, and Peggy Mac-Donald was grinning at her.

"Peggy, I don't care if you do think I'm chicken. I'm not trying it. You can't even see the intersection from here. Who knows how many cars would be zooming along that street when I got to the bottom?"

Peggy laughed back over her shoulder, crouching a little, then shoved herself off, wheels whirring. She swooped down the hill in a broad, swinging flight, her long hair whipping in the wind.

Meg had gulped hard and stiffened her back, wishing she could be more like Peggy—Peggy clambering up trees, Peggy bouncing through the rapids on her inner tube, laughing in the face of danger.

Even the words on Peggy's yellow T-shirt had mocked her. They read, "Why not try?"

For one minute Meg had thought she might do

it. Maybe it would be OK. If you forced yourself to do it once, it wouldn't be so bad the next time. It might not be as risky as it looked. Maybe it would be worth getting hurt, even, if just once she weren't left behind, scared to join in.

She picked up her skateboard and started walking down Mulberry Street. Just beyond the clinic, where the street curved, she could see all the way down to the intersection. Was Peggy down there yet? She looked for the yellow T-shirt. She couldn't—.

Meg gasped. Peggy was sprawled on the grassy boulevard, just short of the intersection. Was she hurt? Meg took off on a dead run, her mouth dry with panic.

"Peggy," she called, "are you all right?"

She had almost reached the figure lying on the grass when she saw some movement. Peggy slowly sat up, then twisted herself around and struggled to her feet. Her jeans were torn, and blood was oozing from her scraped knee, but Peggy still managed a jaunty smile.

"It didn't quite work out," she shrugged. "When I saw two cars wheeling along Grant Street, I figured I'd better grab for a tree, even if I wiped out."

It was Peggy who had taken the spill, but it was Meg who trembled all the way home, thinking about how much worse it could have been.

Peggy took a lot of chances, and somehow for her it all seemed to turn out all right. When this pastor said, "I dare you," maybe he should be talking to somebody more like Peggy.

Sermons usually seemed a little dreary to Meg, but today was different. The young pastor leaned forward, gripping the pulpit. His words painted a picture of Jesus on the mountaintop, weak from hunger, but stronger than the tempter who stood at his elbow.

"The devil offered Jesus a quick, spectacular way to prove something," he said. "The crowds would have loved the show. How quickly the world would have learned about his special powers."

"Go ahead," the devil had suggested. "If you are the Son of God, throw yourself down from the pinnacle of the temple."

Jesus turned him down flat, and Meg began to see why. It was true, what the pastor said. Sometimes it takes more guts to say no.

"Sometimes it's good to be willing to take a risk, but don't let other people make up your mind for you. Take charge of your own life. Choose the risks that are worth taking. Make up your own mind whether an action would be brave or simply showing off." Meg caught herself smiling at the pastor and nodding her head in agreement.

She wasn't at all like Peggy, and probably never would be. Peggy's challenge was her nightmare, and from now on Meg would be brave enough to admit it.

"Then the devil took him to the holy city, and set him on the pinnacle of the temple, and said to him, 'If you are the Son of God, throw yourself down. . . .' Jesus said to him, 'Again it is written, You shall not tempt the Lord your God.'"

Matthew 4:5-6a and 7

Sometimes other kids pressure me to take chances. Lord, show me which risks are worth taking. When no is the best answer, give me the courage to say it. Amen.

I'm No Superkid

I know I'm not doing especially well in school, or in anything else, but how can I get to be the Superkid my folks expect me to be?

Anne Elizabeth tried to sneak into the house through the patio door.

"That you, Anne Elizabeth?"

She frowned at the sound of her mother's voice, then headed toward the laundry chute with her gym clothes. Her mother appeared from nowhere and followed her down the hall. "Well, honey, did you make the cast?" she prodded anxiously.

Anne Elizabeth stuck her nose in the air and fluffed her hair with one hand. "They begged me to take the starring role, but I told them I'd already signed with Universal Studios."

No way was she going to talk with her mother about how hurt she really felt. Even the walk-on roles in the school play had slipped through her fingers.

"Now what does that mean?" her mother asked.

"It means," she snapped, "that I'd just as soon not talk about the play tryouts. All right? The Academy Award will just have to wait for a while."

"Well, Anne Elizabeth, you don't have to. . . ." Mother stopped for a moment, then went on. "Did you get the history papers back?"

Ignoring the question, Anne Elizabeth flipped on the TV switch and plopped down on the sofa, perching her feet up on the back. With the TV going, she could forget about everything for a while. If once, just once, she could do something good enough to please her father and mother! They'd love it if she'd bring home spelling prizes and athletic trophies and blue ribbons for art work. They'd be happy if she could sing solos and star in theater and get all A's in her classes.

"No matter how much I study for something, I couldn't get the best grade," she told herself, "and my folks just wouldn't be proud of anything less. Once I studied three hours for a quiz, and my grade was nothing special."

She hadn't even tried to do well on that history paper. If she had worked really hard and still could only get a C+ on it, she'd know she just wasn't any good, but this way she could always think, "Maybe if I had really tried, I'd have had an A."

The TV drowned out the sounds of the knock at the back door and her mother letting someone into the kitchen. Anne Elizabeth was startled to see their neighbor, Marcy, standing there in her orange and yellow warm-ups and her running shoes.

"Hi. Do me a favor, friend?" Marcy asked.

Anne Elizabeth knew without asking what the favor was. She often watched little Nathan while his mother went out running. Today it was as good a way as any to get away from her mother's questions.

"Sure," she said. "I'll come right over."

What would she do with Nathan today? She always had a pretty good time with the little guy. Maybe today they should model some farm animals out of clay.

Nathan was willing to try. His little fingers dug into the clay and formed something that looked a little like a cow.

Marcy was out of breath when she got back, and her face was red, but she strode briskly around the house, letting herself slow down gradually.

"Only two more weeks before the Midville Marathon," Marcy said, mixing some orange juice in the blender. "I'm not quite in shape yet, but I'm working on it."

"I hope you win," Anne Elizabeth said.

Marcy laughed. "Me? Win? There'll be 300 runners in that marathon."

"But it's a race, isn't it? Why even try, if there's no chance?"

"I'm just not going into it with the idea of winning."

Anne Elizabeth looked puzzled. "I've wondered why people who like to run never give up. I see Mr. Gregory running down River Road every time we go to the Dari-Stop. He really doesn't move very fast, but he just keeps on going. He's getting pretty old, too."

Marcy explained, "It's the running itself that counts, not the winning. It's that wonderful free feeling it gives you. And in a marathon you feel a kind of friendship with everybody sharing the course with you, even those you've never met. You're all in it together, and the race itself is more important than any single runner. And, Anne Elizabeth, it's something else."

"What else?"

"Well, it's an idea, a thing we call our personal best. It's not important to me that I run the best time that's ever been run on that 20-mile course. What is important is that I do a better job than *I've* ever done before. That's my personal best."

Anne Elizabeth sighed. "Every time I do something, I feel like it's my personal worst."

"Hey, what are you talking about?"

"My dad and mom want me to be good at everything, and I'm just not the All-American Kid."

Marcy nodded, then took a long sip of orange juice. "Do you suppose it's because they're disappointed in themselves? Maybe they've always had a secret dream of being a great musician or a star

84

athlete, and maybe they've just realized that they'll never make it. They see you as their own second chance."

"I guess that's it. Maybe when I make a flop of something they feel like they're failing just one more time."

"You know, Anne Elizabeth, all of us are a kind of failure at most things, but that doesn't mean we can't do anything. We just keep on looking until we find the things we do best. Fear of failure keeps us from even trying, and we miss out on all the fun."

Marcy reminded her that failing is one way of learning. "If you misspell a word once and get really mad at yourself about it, you'll probably never misspell that word again."

"Marcy, if I could just know that there was something I could do."

"The magic word is 'try.' Being a kid is a little like a tasting party. You get to try a little bit of this and that before you settle on the dish you like best. But when I say 'try' I mean give it a real chance. One swing of a tennis racket or one saxophone lesson won't give you your answer. Take time to discover what you really like to do." Then she added, "For openers, I know one thing you're really good at."

"Me? You do?" Anne Elizabeth looked surprised.

"Yes, I do. You are the best baby-sitter in the neighborhood. That may mean that you have a natural ability for teaching or nursing or child guidance. Anybody who can make an artist out of Nathan is some kind of a sitter!"

"Sitting," Anne Elizabeth said thoughtfully. "I never thought of that as a talent—like playing guitar or writing poetry or drawing a picture."

"OK," Marcy went on, "that's a beginning." She put her arm around the girl's shoulder. "Anne Elizabeth, promise me two things."

"Two things?"

"Right. First, you'll keep your eye only on your own scorecard."

"OK."

"And promise me that you'll tell your mom and dad how you feel."

"But, Marcy, they won't—"

"Anne Elizabeth, they love you. You must share your feelings with them."

That last promise made Anne Elizabeth nervous. She just picked at her dinner that night. Every time she started to say something, it was like getting up to give an oral report in English. But a promise was a promise. When her dad asked her about the play tryouts, she knew the time had come. She had to tell them how she felt.

She explained about Marcy and the marathon and about how she'd like to do things just for the good feeling of taking part. She asked if they could forget about ribbons and trophies and about her being a star. From now on she just wanted to work toward her personal best.

Mom and Dad looked uncomfortable for a minute. For a little while they said nothing at all. Then she noticed Mom reach over to grip Dad's hand.

"Anne Elizabeth," Dad said, "I guess we were a little mixed up. We just assumed that every kid wants more than anything to be a winner."

Her mother added, "We've both learned that things we do don't always go just the way we want them to. I've never yet made a batch of cookies without at least one sheet-ful getting just a little too brown. We should have known that you're old enough to handle some disappointments, too."

"Anne Elizabeth," her father said, "we'll try to do a lot better. You don't have to prove a thing to your mother and me. From now on, if you're doing your best at something and having a good time doing it, that makes you a winner."

> "But when they measure themselves by one another, and compare themselves with one another, they are without understanding."
>
> 2 Corinthians 10:12b

Lord, help me forget about everyone else's scorecard. Keep my eye fixed only on my personal best. Amen.

A New Dad

Dad died a few years ago, and now Mom says we're going to have a new father. I like Don OK, but I'm kind of worried. I don't even know what I'll call him.

For everybody else in Parker City it was just May 14, a date on the calendar, a morning in spring. But at the Patterson apartment it was the day that would change everything. It was the day of the wedding.

Lynn's excitement weakened her in the gray half-light of dawn. She pressed the button on top of her alarm clock before it could go off, then bounced out of bed and jerked the drapery open all the way. Even the empty street below seemed to be waiting for something to happen. Then Lynn glanced at Lisa, curled up under the covers, hugging her pillow.

Lisa's eyes were shut tight, but one tear was sliding down her cheek beside her nose.

"Lisa, you awake?"

Lisa's chin trembled. "I'm awake," she answered, her voice pinched and miserable. "Well, Lynn, I hope you're happy. Today somebody is coming to take Daddy's place. It's what you've wanted."

"Look, Lisa, I miss Daddy as much as you do. I remember him skipping stones across the pond and pushing the swing as high as it would go. When he died it was the blackest, saddest day of my entire life. But that was three years ago. It's been lonely here. All the other kids have dads to talk to and to help them with things."

Lisa was unconvinced. "Every time Jim comes over you make such a big deal out of it, smiling and bringing him coffee and showing him the stuff from our vacation. It's just dumb."

"Well, Lisa, you don't even give him a chance. Whenever he's invited us someplace you've been too busy to go. When you do talk to him you say about two words."

There was a soft knock, and the door opened. Mother stood there in her yellow housecoat. "OK if I come in for a minute?"

She was carrying the big picture of Daddy, the one in the gold frame that always stood on her dresser.

"I thought you girls might like to have Daddy's picture in your room," she said, setting it on the desk.

Lisa's forehead hardened into a frown. She turned her face to the wall.

"Lisa, honey," Mom began, "we all miss Daddy. We'll always love him, you know that. He'll always be a part of us. But I'm going to be married to Jim now. It wouldn't be fair to him if I kept the picture there. Can you understand?"

Lisa lay motionless. It was Lynn who said, "It'll be OK, Mom. It will be just perfect. We'll have a whole family again."

Mom looked at her gently and shook her head.

"Lynn, Lynn, slow down a minute, will you? Ever since I started dating you've been running down the hall to meet every elevator. Your cheerleader's welcome almost scared Jim away. It takes time for two people to decide on marriage. I wanted to be sure I wasn't marrying just to find a father for you two or just to have help with the house. I didn't want you to push me into it."

Lisa sat up and flung the blanket back. "You're so sure it will be perfect," she snapped at her sister. "You can't know that, Lynn. You can't know that at all."

Mom sat down on the bed beside her. "I agree with you, Lisa."

Lisa looked at her in surprise.

"None of us can know that for sure, can we?" Mom went on. "But Lynn has been lonely for a long time. It's like she's been carrying a picture around inside her, the dream of a new father who might make us as happy as Daddy did. The trouble is, the dream father is so good that nobody could live up to it, certainly not Jim. He's really nice, but he's not perfect."

"You know that, Mom?" Lisa asked.

"Right. And, you know, he's been carrying a picture around with him, too, a picture of the wife and children he'd like to have someday. He's told me that. But he'll have to learn that we all have faults, too. There'll be days when his dream family will look like a pretty poor bargain."

"But what about Daddy? How can we just forget him?"

"I haven't told you this before, Lisa, but it's all right with Daddy."

"All right with . . . him?" The words came slowly. How could Mom know that?

"Yes. Just before he died, Daddy was worried about all of us. He told me then he hoped I'd find somebody else who would be good to me and would help take care of you."

"It's . . . all right . . . with Daddy." Lisa sat quietly, lost in thought.

"And, Lisa, it's all right with God, too. You remember the wedding vows say 'until death do us part.' They mean just that. God's Word is clear. A widow or widower is free to marry again. Jim and I have prayed about it. It's important to us to have God's blessing. We think we have our answer. It's all right with God."

"It's all right with Daddy and all right with God."

Lisa's eyes were swimming with unshed tears. Her mother laid a hand on her hair.

"But, Lisa, this could be a beautiful day if it were all right with you, too."

"I think maybe it'll be OK now." Lisa's voice was muffled. "But, Mom, I don't really feel like Jim is a part of our family. Do you want us to fake it?"

"Of course not. We all have to be honest about our feelings."

Mom reached over and picked the green leather photo album off the bookshelf, opening it to the first page.

"Look, Lisa, this is the way you looked the day we brought you home from the hospital—our beautiful new baby. We were excited, and we were beginning to feel like your parents, but we didn't love you that day as much as we learned to love you later on."

"You mean you had to learn to love me?"

"Sure. The more we took care of you, the more we loved you. We loved you even more after we had all built up a collection of good memories."

"Are you saying it would be all right if I gradually learned to love Jim?"

Lynn grinned at that. "Why not? Everybody doesn't have to throw rose petals in his path like me. We can get to be a family in stages."

Their mother flipped the plastic-coated pages of the album, her eyes softening with memories of school plays and picnics and camping trips. "Jim is only beginning to build up his memory collection," she mused.

Now it was Lynn who said, "But, Mom, Lisa and I have had all of your attention. Can you love us as much from now on? Even I worry about that sometimes."

Mother's answer was firm. "Love isn't like a watermelon, you know. If you give one person a slice, that doesn't mean there's one less helping for somebody else. It's more like one of my houseplants. When I snip off a cutting to give to a friend, my own plant just grows stronger and fuller and gives more blossoms. The more love you give somebody, the more you have left to give. Loving Jim will make me happier, so I'll have even more love to give to both of you."

Lisa was sliding the hangers along the closet pole, finding the new dress Mom had bought her for the wedding.

"One more question," she said, her voice steady now. "What'll we call him?"

"You'll call him whatever makes you feel comfortable," her mother assured her. "I would think you'd always save the name Daddy for the father you loved first, when you were a little girl. Certainly the name Jim is all right for a while . . . and forever, if that's what feels good to you. If you decide later he's become a father to you, you might try Father or Dad."

Mother added, "I don't think I'd like to hear you use the word 'stepfather.' It's an old-fashioned term that reminds me of cruel people in the old fairy tales. And maybe Jim would feel better if you didn't refer to Daddy as your real father, as if his own tie with you were not a real one. You can certainly have two fathers, both of them real."

"I think it might work. Thanks for letting me take my time." Lisa wrapped her arms around her mother in a hug.

> "For when they rise from the dead, they neither marry nor are given in marriage, but are like angels in heaven."
>
> Mark 12:25

Sometimes, Father, we have to learn to love each other. We keep building walls, but teach us just to let love happen. Amen.

God Seems a Little Scary

Sometimes I'm afraid because of something scary I've seen on TV. Other times I can't stop thinking about dying. I even worry about God. How can I get over it?

Heidi lay in the dark, her eyes wide open. Warmth from her body had made an island of comfort in the sheets, but she couldn't get to sleep. She kept thinking about the same things that had kept her awake last night, and the night before.

Ever since Aunt Barbara died, the same troublesome questions kept coming back. They didn't bother her in her daytime world of hamburgers and homework and flute lessons. But at night, in the dark, she couldn't stop thinking about them.

"If Aunt Barbara is supposed to be in heaven, why

did they put her in the ground? . . . They tell me she died because she was so sick. Well, Kevin is sick right now. Is he going to die?"

Grandma had explained that God loved Aunt Barb so much he took her to heaven. "He loves me, too," Heidi had thought. "Where is he planning to take me? To tell the truth, I hope he doesn't like me that much."

If only the house weren't so quiet. Mom's friend Jan was visiting them, but she had gone to bed early, and now Heidi's parents had gone to their room. For a while she had heard them talking, but now it was perfectly still. The ear that Heidi had pressed against her pillow made a little thumping sound. That bothered her, too, so she rolled over on her back.

Why didn't bedtime prayers make Heidi feel safe anymore? Lately she didn't even want to think about God. If only he were just a plain person, somebody with a face and a handshake. But God was invisible, and God could see inside of her, and how could God be both here and in Indianapolis at the same time?

Then Heidi would begin to feel sort of wicked for thinking such thoughts. Her folks and her teachers and her pastor wanted her to have faith and not to ask so many questions.

Heidi shivered. She walked boldly to the wall switch. Light flooded the room. Shadowy corners that had threatened her awhile ago were all right now. The chair was there, and the desk—the posters and hairbrush and pencil holder.

She went into the bathroom and turned on the warm water, then held her hand under it. The tight feeling in her scalp began to loosen its grip. She breathed more easily.

Light and water couldn't answer her questions, but they could give her back her plain, everyday feelings. Her fears melted away like ice cream in a hot dish. Light was something you could see. Wetness was something you could feel. They weren't like the far-away, invisible God.

Before trying to sleep again, maybe she should eat something. She hardly ever thought about unexplainable things when she was biting into a sandwich or swallowing chocolate milk.

Heidi walked lightly past the other bedrooms and quietly opened the kitchen door. She screwed the lid off a jar and scooped a soft, circular path through the peanut butter with a knife. As she pulled open the door of the bread box, she heard a sound behind her and looked up into the smiling eyes of Mom's friend, Jan.

"I couldn't sleep, either," Jan explained. "Could I get in on the party?"

Jan mixed chocolate milk while Heidi put together another peanut butter sandwich. Then they sat down at the butcher-block table to eat.

"Tell me, Heidi," Jan said, "what keeps a girl your age awake at this time of night?"

Heidi wouldn't have told most adults about her feelings, but suddenly she knew it might help to tell Jan. She started to talk to her about Aunt Barbara.

She recalled how she had felt standing by the open coffin. It was as if death had erased Aunt Barbara and left this sleeping stranger in her place. Her freckles were covered up, and those smile crinkles at the corners of her eyes. Springy brown hair had been tamed into orderly waves. Her once-quick hands had been placed together, rigid and still.

Then Heidi told Jan about the questions Aunt Barbara's death had raised. Jan nodded thoughtfully.

"And ever since your Aunt Barbara died you've been afraid that everyone else will die, too. Maybe her death is even a reminder that you're going to die some day."

"True. I get really scared, Jan. And that isn't even the worst part."

"Don't tell me. I'll bet I know. I'll bet Aunt Barbara's death makes you feel angry, too—angry with God."

Heidi didn't even dare to look at Jan. How did she know?

"Have you talked with God about it?"

"No."

"Is that any way to treat a friend?"

Heidi sighed. "I know we're all supposed to love God and be his friend, but I'm not sure I can do it."

"What is God like, Heidi?"

"Well, that's hard to explain. To me he's really mysterious."

Jan looked straight at her. "And maybe even scary?"

"Yes, scary. He's invisible, and he can see inside me and know what I'm thinking and. . . ."

"Well, you know there are mysteries and mysteries," Jan explained. "There are mystery books that make you sick with fear. But a really good mystery book can be like a neat riddle. It's fun trying to figure things out."

"Yes," Heidi agreed. "The only mystery books I really like are those where you expect to learn the answers some time, but not quite yet."

"Exactly!" Jan said. "Some things about God are hidden from us. The Bible tells us that now we see God through a mirror darkly, but some day we'll meet him face to face. There's mystery about God, but he's not spooky."

After a big swallow of chocolate milk, Heidi confessed, "It's wrong, but I keep asking myself questions about God."

"God doesn't mind if you try to figure him out. That's what all of the great religious thinkers do. You're angry with God because Barbara died. Well, tell him so."

Heidi frowned. "I wouldn't dare tell God I'm mad at him."

"Why not? The man who wrote the Psalms did that. So did Moses. God wants you to be honest about your feelings."

"He does?"

"Once you know what God is like, Heidi, talking to him is as easy as spreading peanut butter. You can just dump out all your thoughts without sorting them. God will sort them for you. I'll bet you think God always expects you to show up in your Sunday dress."

Heidi laughed at that. "That's about right. Isn't God like that?"

Jan shook her head. "I think God likes you just fine in your blue jeans. One of the big reasons Jesus came to earth was to show us what God is like. How did Jesus act around people?"

"Well, he listened to the children."

"And he'll listen to you. He was the kind of a person who cared about hungry people and made sick people well again. Does that sound scary?"

"Well, no, but—"

"You're comfortable with your friends because you talk to them every day. God would like to be that kind of friend to you, too, Heidi. You've been afraid of God because you know he can see what's inside of you, right?"

"Right. If I so much as think a bad thing, he knows about it."

"But if he really knows you inside, he can see how hard you're trying. You can count on him. In our life after death, we'll be safe forever with a strong and gentle friend."

Heidi's eyes were beginning to look drowsy. She picked up her glass and carried it to the sink. "Thanks for our talk, Jan. I guess God isn't so scary after all. Now I think I'll say my prayers over and get to sleep."

> "For now we see in a mirror dimly, but then face to face."
>
> 1 Corinthians 13:12a

I can't see you yet, Jesus, but I can know you. Every day I can talk with you. Thanks for coming to show me what God is like. Until all my questions are answered and I can see your face, keep me safe in your love. Amen.

It Isn't Fair

The fight never would have happened if my brother hadn't started it, but Mom treated me as if it was all my fault. I didn't know she could be so unfair.

"It isn't fair. It just isn't fair!" Betsy flung herself across her bed. Grabbing her pillow as she flipped over on her back, she punched her fist into it, over and over.

Mother hadn't been in on the whole thing. She just came into the kitchen and saw Benjie standing there with water dripping down his shirt, hollering his head off.

Benjie had asked for it. All morning he had been bothering her. Nobody had asked him to come around when Gail came over, listening in on everything and wiggling his loose tooth to show off.

It was Benjie who had messed around with her Monopoly set and lost most of the little houses. She could have strangled him for getting up early and turning on the TV just so she wouldn't get to choose the channel.

And now this business about the water. She had been carrying the ice-cube tray across the kitchen, trying to hold it steady so she wouldn't spill. If Benjie had had his eyes open he would have seen what she was trying to do, but he came charging through from outside and bumped into her arm. Maybe it was kind of mean throwing the rest of the water all over his shirt, but Benjie had been asking for it all morning, and Mother didn't have to act like everything was her fault.

When he started hollering, "Betsy threw water on me, Betsy threw water on me," Mother had come storming into the kitchen and sent Betsy to her room.

Benjie didn't even have to go to his room. As soon as he had a dry shirt on, Mom had let him go outside to play. He was even bouncing a ball against the house right outside her window, as if to remind her that he had won.

Betsy thought that Gail was lucky, not having any little brothers to cause problems. This wasn't the first time Benjie had gotten his own way because Mother babied him. Why did little kids have to get all the breaks? She hadn't asked to be born first.

"Betsy?" Mother knocked at her door. "Mind if I come in? I need to talk with you for a minute."

"Go away, will you, Mother? You told me to go to

my room. Now I just want to be here by myself. Just go away."

There was silence, then the sound of footsteps, walking away.

Betsy tuned her radio in to the Top 40 station, a little louder than necessary, then lay twisting the fringe on her bedspread. Gradually her rage and frustration began to ooze away.

That night at supper Dad said to Mother, "You seem tired, dear. You all right?"

Mother glanced at Betsy, then quickly back to Dad. "It's been a hard day for all of us. The wash machine quit on me just when I was doing all the bedroom curtains. Then the man from Foster's called and said that wallpaper we ordered is out of stock, and I've been worried about who to line up for that committee assignment. Now I'm afraid Betsy and I are having some trouble."

Betsy just sat there rolling a meatball around in the gravy, saying nothing.

"Betsy, what have you done?"

Now Dad's doing the same thing. What have *I* done? Maybe it would be better just to stay quiet.

Dad looked toward Benjie. "Benjie, can you help me out?"

Benjie was busy with his knife, digging butter into his bran muffin.

"Me?" he said, not looking up. "Well, I guess Betsy got so mad at me for bumping into her that she threw water all over me."

"And he pestered Gail and me, and he lost my

Monopoly pieces, and he hogged the TV all morning, and I'm the one who had to spend a whole hour in my room like a prisoner. Benjie started it all, but I'm the one who got punished. It isn't fair. It just isn't fair. . . . May I be excused?"

She got to her feet, but Dad stopped her. "Betsy, you stay right there."

Startled by the firmness in his voice, she slid quietly back into her chair.

"I want you and Benjie to settle some things between the two of you before you leave this table."

Mother broke in. "How about the three of us?" she said. "For one thing, I guess I owe Betsy an apology. I really didn't take time to get the facts straight before I sent her off to her room, and I'm sorry about that."

"Well," Betsy conceded, "I suppose maybe you just wanted to shut off the noise."

"That's about it. I didn't really care who started the fight. I just wanted to end it. It was really your problem and Benjie's, but the noise and the puddle of water on the floor suddenly made it my business, too."

Dad looked at Betsy and Benjie. "You're finding out that it isn't easy, being a perfect kid?" They both nodded. "Well,'" he added, "it's at least that hard being a perfect parent."

Thoughtfully, Mother announced, "I think what I'd really like to do is to offer my resignation."

"Your resignation?'" Benjie shook his head in disbelief. "Mothers can't just quit, can they?"

Mother laughed. "Not as a mother. I love being your mother, Benjie, but I've about had it with the referee's job."

"Referee?" Betsy didn't quite understand.

"Yes. I'm so busy blowing the whistle for your fights that I don't get more important things done."

Dad asked, "How do you kids in the neighborhood settle things when you're playing out in the vacant lot? You don't have umpires or referees there, do you?"

"No," Benjie answered. "We just sort of figure it out for ourselves."

Betsy added, "Of course, we have rules there, and we just try to use those to settle the fights. That helps."

"What would be so bad about setting up some rules around here?" Dad wondered. "Maybe you could think of a way to get Mother off the hook."

"I know a good one," Betsy offered. "I think a cooling-off period might help. You know, just separate ourselves for a while before we even try to settle it. I guess Mother had the right idea today, but the thing I didn't like was that I was the only one sent away to cool off."

"Sure," Benjie agreed. "We could both go off someplace. It'd have to be that way, because if we were arguing about TV channels both of us would want to stay right there with the TV for the cooling off. We'd both like the other one to go away."

"OK. Cooling-off period. What else?" Betsy was serious about the rules.

Benjie said, "Couldn't we have one about reaching an agreement before the next meal? I really hate leftover fights for dinner. It wrecks my appetite."

"Yeah, a time limit seems like a good idea," Betsy said. "Even when I'm enjoying a fight, I want it to end sometime. I've heard on the news about labor disputes, and they have lists of grievances. That sounds pretty neat. I could write down what makes me mad and you could write down what makes you mad. It might help."

"OK. I'm sure I could think of lots of grievances," Benjie agreed.

"Maybe it would even be a good idea if we'd list the stuff that we've done wrong ourselves. It would be hard to do, but if the rules said we had to, it might help. Today in my room I could remember right away all the mean things Benjie had done, but after I cooled off a little I admitted to myself that I might have done a few things, too—like throwing out Benjie's rocks because I wanted to use the blue plastic pail and because I didn't think the rocks looked very important."

"Let him who is without sin cast the first stone," Dad mused.

"Let what?" Benjie said.

"Well, you know, Jesus had a pretty good way of making people take a good look at themselves. An angry mob was getting ready to throw stones at a sinner, and the Lord forced them to think again. He invited anybody who had never done anything wrong to throw the first stone at her."

Betsy grinned. "That was a great way to handle it. Y'know, I think our rules might work. I suppose we'll need some more, but at least we've got a start. I'll write down those we have so far. OK, Benjie?"

"OK. Now couldn't we talk about something else? Mom, what's for dessert?"

> "For there is no distinction; since all have sinned and fall short of the glory of God."
>
> Romans 3:22b-23

To be honest, God, I'm not perfect. When there's a fight it's hard to admit that I'm partly to blame. Nobody can be perfect, not even parents. Help us all to get along and to like each other, faults and all. Amen.

Come as You Are

I did something wrong, and I don't think I'll ever feel good about myself again. I can't seem to live up to God's laws. Do you suppose I'm not even a Christian?

Margit stood in the shower, her fingers digging into her scalp as she worked her hair into a foamy cloud. Why had she said it? Dad had kept talking and talking about her math grades, and her anger had built to the bursting point. Suddenly she had heard herself shouting at him, hollering things like he didn't care about her and all he thought about was report cards and letting everybody know how smart his daughter was.

For a while it felt like she had won. Dad dropped the subject and picked up his paper. Things quieted down around the house. Standing under the shower with the spray of warm water had always given her a clean, happy feeling, but today there were other feelings that stuck to her like a tattoo. They wouldn't wash away.

"Honor thy father and thy mother." The words from the Bible sounded stiff and stern and old-fashioned, but they kept popping into her mind. Margit was uneasy as she dried herself and put on clean jeans and a ragged gray sweatshirt. Her hair dripping in uncombed strings, she draped a towel over her shoulders and walked through the living room. Her dad frowned into his paper, and Margit could think of no words to break through the quietness.

Then the doorbell rang once, twice. Margit drew the big towel up around her head like a turban, wet fringes of hair still dripping out around the edges, and went to the door.

"You're perfect!" Gretchen almost shrieked as she opened the door.

"Perfect?" Margit shook her head. She clutched the clumsy towel around her head and let Gretchen into the hall.

Gretchen grinned. "No fooling, Margit. You'll look neat for the come-as-you-are party."

"Party? You're kidding!"

"Nope. We're all getting together at Martha's house. Her mom has fixed some stuff to eat, and Martha's figured out some games, but you can't get yourself fixed up. You just have to drop everything and come with me—just like you are."

"Gretchen, there aren't—"

"No, don't worry. No boys. Quite a few girls are already there. Come on."

"It's OK, Margit. I'll tell Mother," Dad called out to her.

The party was fun. Mary had come with only one shoe, and Trisha had poster paint all over her hands. The hem of Sherry's skirt was pinned up halfway around.

Margit came home in the late afternoon, full of pizza and popcorn and happier feelings. Dad seemed to have forgotten about the fight, and Margit forgot about it, too, until bedtime.

Sleep wouldn't come. She lay there for a long time, thinking. She loved Dad. She wanted to get along with him. Then why did she say those ugly things?

Margit got out of bed, put on her robe and slippers, and padded down the carpeted stairs. Dad was sitting by the fire alone.

"Dad?" she said tentatively.

"Having trouble getting to sleep, honey?" he asked.

"Yeah. I can't get it off my mind—those things I hollered at you. Now I guess I'd like to feel good about myself again."

"Maybe we both could use a little forgiveness." He picked up a poker and moved the glowing log on the grate. "Looks like we've got two problems, forgiving each other and being sure God forgives us both."

"That's it, Dad. I want to be a Christian, but I keep doing it all wrong."

"Margit, maybe it would help to think of life as a kind of come-as-you-are party."

"A what?"

"Well, you know—like Martha's party today. It was a great idea, wasn't it?"

"Well, yes, but—"

"Think about it a minute. Our Lord spent a lot of his time on earth passing out come-as-you-are invitations."

"He did?"

"Sure. Mary Magdalene had a pretty bad reputation, but the first thing Jesus did was to love her just as she was. Then he gave her a chance to become better."

Dad added, "And when he chose his disciples, he didn't say they couldn't join him till after they had learned to handle their bad tempers or after they became more honest."

"Nope," Margit agreed, "all he really said was 'Follow me.'"

"And, Margit, do you remember Zacchaeus?"

Margit laughed. "How could I forget Zacchaeus? Remember how Billy fell out of the tree when he was Zacchaeus in the Sunday school play? The step ladder tipped over."

Dad nodded. "I remember. But you know that the real Zacchaeus came down from the tree for a better reason. Zacchaeus was a crooked tax collector, but Jesus invited him to come as he was and to be the

114

host at a dinner party. Zacchaeus couldn't believe Jesus would honor him that way.

"Y'know, Dad, when I think about what God would like me to be, I'm really ashamed. I'm not even sure I'm a Christian."

"Margit, every Christian is both a sinner and a saint. All of us do wrong things, but we're saints because God's power is working in us, moving us toward something better. Nobody ever said it would be easy. What's important is that we know the invitation still stands: Come as you are.

"I have an invitation, too, Margit. Jesus sees me as I am—a dad who pushes too hard about grades. You're much more important to me than a report card, but sometimes I forget to tell you so."

Margit stood there for a long moment, looking into the red and gray coals of the dying fire. Then she walked over to the easy chair and planted a kiss on her father's forehead.

"Good night, Dad," she said. "I think I can sleep now."

"Good night, Margit. Thank you for sharing your feelings."

> "Not that I have already obtained this or am already perfect; but I press on."
>
> Philippians 3:12

Thank you, Jesus, for the come-as-you-are invitation. Your forgiveness makes me feel comfortable and good. Amen.

First Aid for Friendship

My best friend and I had a fight, and we're not even talking to each other. To tell the truth, I'd like to be friends again, but I can't figure out how.

"I'll call you in the morning, Dad," Jody promised, slamming the tailgate of the wagon. Then she staggered up the walk, loaded down with sleeping bag, pillow, record albums, and food.

"Let me help you with that, Jody," Michele's mother offered as she let her in. "Are you sure you're planning to stay just overnight?"

"C'mon up, Jody. We're in my room," Michele hollered down the stairs.

A grin spread over Jody's round face as she followed a blast of music and laughter up to Michele's room. She had always liked that room—yellow, checked gingham at the windows, a squashy, saucer-eyed panda plopped in the middle of the canopy bed, yellow and green shelves filled with Michele's books and treasures.

But tonight she scarcely noticed. Sleeping bags carpeted the floor. Crackling bags of corn crisps and pretzels, soft drink cans, records, and hair rollers were all scrambled together in pleasant confusion. There were girls talking and laughing and snapping gum, prancing around in stocking feet, sitting cross-legged on the floor, lying across the bed.

Jody liked Michele. Other kids might plan a picnic and leave her out, but never Michele. You could tell Michele a secret and she didn't run around blabbing it to everybody else. Other kids laughed at Jody for being overweight and clumsy at games, but Michele always picked her for her side.

Michele looked out the window. "Guess what! There's a full moon," she said. "Why don't we all put on jackets and boots and go out and play Fox and Geese?"

Soon they had tramped off a big circle in the snow and were jogging after each other in breathless pursuit. Later, pink-cheeked and exhausted, they piled into the kitchen for doughnuts and hot cocoa.

It would have been bedtime at home, but tonight was different. Getting into pajamas meant that the night was just beginning. For a while they all listened to one another's records. Then Jeanne offered to take charge of a séance, if they felt brave enough.

"I'm sick of that spooky stuff. Let's do Truth Dare,

Double Dare, Promise to, Repeat," Jessie suggested, and soon they were taking turns proving themselves to all the others.

At first Jody thought it was fun, watching the other girls squirm, but then her own turn came.

"Who's your boyfriend, Jody?" came the question from Krista. Suddenly Jody didn't like the game anymore. She'd face any Truth Dare but that one. She could feel her face getting fiery hot. "I can't. I just can't. If he ever found out, I'd die," she protested.

But the others weren't giving up that easily. Everybody was looking at her, waiting. Jody grabbed her pillow, lifted it over her head, and heaved it through the air. Krista ducked, and the pillow crashed against the yellow and green shelves above the desk. Oh, no! Michele's music box with the ceramic angels lay in pieces all over the desk top.

Michele picked up the fragments of an angel, her face tight with disappointment. She turned on Jody. "Now look what you've done. My music box is ruined."

"Oh, Michele," Jody's voice was hushed. "Michele, I didn't mean to—"

"How would you like it if I came to your house and wrecked your doll collection?" Michele shot back.

"But you know it was an—"

"It was stupid and clumsy." Michele set the pieces of the music box down on the desk. "Thanks a lot, Fatso."

Fatso! Jody couldn't believe what she was hearing. Other kids had called her by that ugly name, but now it was Michele. Jody was engulfed by a mixture of feelings—rage, disappointment, embarrassment. Then her own words poured out in a fierce, biting flood.

Suddenly Jody knelt down on her knees and began to roll up her sleeping bag, gulping to force back the sobs. She tied up the lumpy bundle, peeled off her pajamas, and put her clothes back on. Grabbing the other things that belonged to her, she stomped down the stairs to the telephone.

It was awful the following Monday. When Michele got on the school bus, Jody couldn't even look at her. When Michele handed out paper in art class, she thrust a sheet toward Jody, looking the other way.

Each day the silence grew more bristly. Jody couldn't stand it. Michele had always been her best friend. Now they were enemies. All Jody wanted was to have things back the way they were, but each girl waited for the other to break the silence.

"I guess somebody has to make the first move," Jody thought. "Should I? But Michele won't even look at me. Maybe in a couple of days it'll be easier to talk to her."

But Jody knew that was stalling. The longer she waited, the harder it got. Pretty soon things were so bad it seemed like it would take an international peace conference to straighten it all out.

How had it happened? She decided to write it all down. No matter how miserable it made her feel, she would remember all she could about the fight so she would be sure what the problems were.

Well, there was the music box of course, but maybe the real beginning was when everybody at the slumber party got so tired, first running out in the snow, then staying up late.

"When I'm tired I always get sort of touchy and cranky. Do you suppose that's what happens to Michele, too?"

Then there was that dumb game. Talking about boys was hard for Jody. Her embarrassment about that was the real reason she had thrown the pillow, and if she hadn't thrown the pillow Michele would still have her music box, and she and Michele would still be friends.

Jody wrote it all down, even the mean things they both had said. Somehow when it was down on paper, each thing seemed somewhat less serious.

First something would have to be done about the broken music box. Jody decided she could use her paper route money to buy another one, and then maybe Michele would know how sorry she really was.

Ugly words were bigger trouble. It wouldn't be easy to tell Michele how sorry she was and to ask for forgiveness, but Jody knew it would have to be done.

Jody could almost hear the soft voice of her church school teacher, Mrs. Prentice: "If God asks us even to love our enemies, then surely he would like us to forgive our friends."

Jody looked again at the paper, then folded it and put it into her pocket. She had made up her mind. She would make the first move. And stalling wouldn't help. No matter how hard it was, it had to be tomorrow.

When she got on the school bus the next morning, she walked to the first double seat, slid to the window side, and piled her books on the other half to save it.

When Michele got on, she began to walk quickly toward the back, turning her head so she wouldn't have to look at Jody. But Jody leaned way over and pulled at her sleeve.

"I saved a place for you, Michele," she blurted out.

Michele looked startled, then uneasy, but she stopped, half-smiled, and sat down beside her.

Jody's words tumbled out. "Michele, I've got it figured out. I think if I collect for my paper route just one more week, I'll have enough so I can buy you a new music box. I'm sorry I was so careless."

"I knew you were. I liked the music box, Jody, but it shouldn't have been that big a deal."

"Well, will it be OK if I get you a new one?"

"Sure, Jody, that would be fine. But that's the easiest part. There's no way I can buy back those dumb things I said to you."

"Well, once the battle got going I said a few dumb things of my own," Jody said. "Maybe we're even. They sort of cancel each other out, don't you think?"

Michele smiled, a real smile this time. She was

herself again. "It's forgotten, Jody. Could we start over?"

"OK, Michele, why not?"

> "As the Lord has forgiven you, so you also must forgive."
>
> Colossians 3:13b

Many times, Jesus, I have come to you for forgiveness. Now it is my turn to forgive my friend. Show me how to do it gladly. Amen.